Toward

A Short Story Collection by
H. Troy Green

Inglenook Press
Petersburg, Tennessee

Copyright © 2017 H. Troy Green

All rights reserved. This book or any portion thereof may not be reproduced or used in any manner whatsoever without the express written permission of the publisher except for the use of brief quotations in a book review.

Cover illustration and internal illustrations Copyright © 2017 by H. Troy Green.

Cover illustration and design by A. McKenzie Green. mckenziegreendesign.com

Editing by Cindy Phiffer.

Thank you for your support!

To sign up for our newsletter and obtain bonus content, visit the author's website at: https://htroygreen.com/

These stories are works of fiction. Names, characters, businesses, places, events and incidents are either the products of the author's imagination or used in a fictitious manner. Any resemblance to actual persons, living or dead, or actual events is purely coincidental.

Contents

Preface	iv
Introduction	vi
Toward	3
Lost	9
Blackberry	25
Clouds	35
Bones	45
Post	59
Guest	65
Crazy	77
Envelope	83
Exit	89
Blue Hydrangea	105
Fields	113
Attention	125
Liberation	131
Last	145
Riverside	163
About the Author	174

Preface

When you start a walk with God you can never be sure precisely where you will end up, but it will be remarkable with points of grace and growth all along the way.

Sometime back I felt those gentle nudges of the Holy Spirit to write stories. What you hold now are some of the ones that seemed to fit a theme of movement, turning, and growth, hence the title *Toward*. And as much as the stories are about moving, the whole process has also been about that for me:

- To sit down and start with just a spark and then be amazed something worth reading developed.
- To have no idea of what it takes to get something published and to have support and encouragement come from so many sources.
- To need help with initial reading, proofing, and editing and have talented and generous people volunteer. It might be my name on the book, but many others played a part to bring *Toward* into existence.

There are many people to thank, but I'll begin with my beautiful wife Margie who really has been nothing but supportive of me in this adventure of artful fiction. My daughter McKenzie designed the cover, and with all things McKenzie, did it perfectly and slowly. But I wouldn't have it any other way. My teen son Harrison encouraged me with reverse psychology, but I know his tricks.

My alpha and beta readers really helped me improve the quality of these stories and gave me practice at being a recipient of grace. Special thanks are due to Angie, Bryan, Cindy (editor), Donna, Elizabeth, Linda, and Michael for their detailed and constructive feedback. Each of you not only helped polish these stories, you improved the writer.

Right now a thunderstorm is rumbling around in the yard. A heavy and welcome rain is providing some white noise. It's great weather for writing or reading. It also demonstrates the wisdom and love of God who created a world with change, seasons and movement—where we are now is not where we will always be!

There are regular days to be spent without awareness of their immense value, dark times of trouble and pain that should not be borne alone, and unimagined moments of joy and love. For all these things and more, I thank Jesus Christ. My prayer for you is that you would know the peace and power of His presence whatever the season of your life.

HTG
Petersburg, Tennessee
August 2017

Introduction

This collection of stories orbits around those unpredictable but defining moments of decision. It is fascinating why people choose and act the way we do. How does one person overcome a mountain of fear and go against a lifetime of training to grow, while another person with half the challenge and twice the support finds themselves unable to get off the merry-go-round?

These brief stories all have realistic settings, characters and points of conflict. To facilitate the movement of the drama and the impact of the resolutions, the prose is not heavy nor elaborate. Most are set in the contemporary South, and the characters range from schoolgirls to old men and face challenges from gardening to suicidal isolation. More than a couple come to surprising endings.

It is my hope that casual readers will be entertained, engaged, and amused, and that careful readers will be moved, delighted, and challenged with a taste of truth. Avid readers might be tempted to read them all in one setting, but like a good sampler of chocolates the most enjoyment will come to those willing to slow down and savor. Each was written so that readers not only observe actions and events, but also participate in the processes at play. So take a moment, find a quiet place, and join in the journey that is *Toward*.

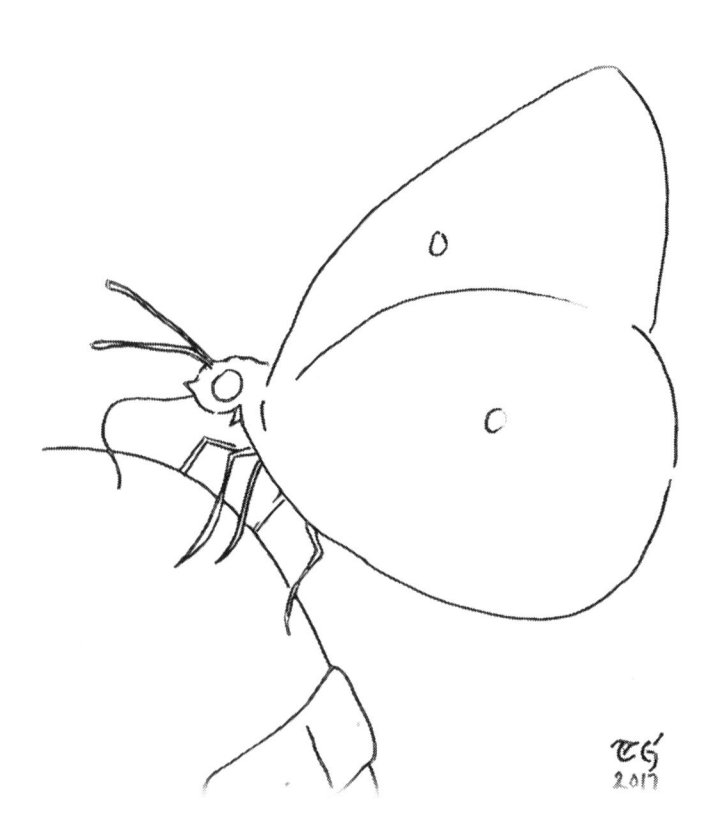

Toward

"Look! There's a flutterfly on my knee!"
"Yes, it is a Cloudless Sulphur."
"It's licking me with its tongue."
"It is a proboscis."
"A proboscis?"
"A straw-like appendage used to draw fluids into its body."
"Are you always so serious, Jenna?"
"No, I am not always so serious."

I look at my best friend Jenna whose name is the same as mine 'cept for one letter and that it doesn't sound the same. I am Lee-na, and she is Jen-a. Jenna is the smartest kid in the third grade—probably the smartest kid in the whole school—but I'm just Lenna.

Jenna is pretty but not really. I like her though for some reason.

I say, "How you know all that stuff?"

She looks at me with her eyelids half closed—checking me out. "I'm just asking," I say.

"I don't know. I just know. I mean I guess I read stuff and remember. I remember what I read. Somewhere I read—it was in Mrs. Stevenson's Encyclopedia of Bugs—that that light yellow-green butterfly with triangle shaped wings is a Cloudless Sulphur."

The flutterfly still sits on my knee. I look up at the sky. It's recess, and we are in our favorite place on the short monkey bars. Nobody likes these monkey bars 'cause they are for little kids. But we don't use them to play on—it'd be too easy to climb—but we like 'em cause we can sit and talk in private. Usually. Sometimes boys come over. I don't mind Henry Marambio, but Ernest Phelps gets on my nerves.

"They call it 'Cloudless' cause it's all one color?" I ask.

Jenna looks up at the sky too, and I see the blue in her glasses and smudges. She says, "Yes, I suppose that might be why. But the book didn't say."

"Yeah. That's probably why. Cause it's clear as a cloudless sky."

"Maybe."

"Of course it is." I say loud but not mean loud. But you know like, I stand up and put my hands out like, "Yeah. Of course." She sees me standing there balancing on the little plastic circles that hold the bars together. I'm good at keeping my balance. She won't stand up though. It took me a forever to get her to crawl up this far.

"So, we have us a mystery," I say real serious. "We got part of the name solved, but what does sull-fer mean?"

Jenna goes with me, and that's why we are friends. We go together. She goes, "So, sulphur is a mineral—"

I cut her off because she answers everything too quick, and then there is no fun in that. At all. "Oh, a mineral. Like maybe the scientist guy—"

Then it was her turn to cut me off, "Or girl!"

"Yeah, ok," I say, "Maybe this scientist girl discovered these flutterflies like to eat sulphur!"

"No, no. That's not it—"

"And she studied all the things they did, from caterpillar to cocoon to flutterfly, and discovered their whole life was about sulphur."

Jenna stares at me and sits up. It's hard to sit up on those bars because it's a balance thing. She rolls her eyes at me anyway.

I put my chin out like I'm pointing down at her and put my hands on my hips. I wobble a little, but I ain't scared.

"And what, may I ask, is wrong with bugs eating sulphur?"

"Sulphur is like rocks or powder, and it stinks."

"It stinks?"

"Yes, sulphur smells like rotten eggs."

"OH!" I can't help but shout, "That's why flutterflies like cow poop!"

She laughs a little and then says, "That's why that one liked licking your knee!"

We laugh so hard we nearly fall off this dad-gummed thing. Then the bell rings, and Miss Violet says, "Come on! Time to go back inside."

We usually just scooch down on our back sides, but I stand up again and hold out my hands to Jenna the genius. She knows what I mean.

"Come on. You can do it."

She needs some 'vincing. I say, "I'll hold you."

Her eyes get big and she looks back toward Miss Violet, but I know we got time for this before Miss Violet uses her serious voice on us. "C'mon," I say.

She gets on her hands and knees and for a second I think she's gonna climb down; then, she holds up a hand. I take it and get my feet more steady.

"So, why did this scientist girl call it Sulphur if it ain't because they eat it?"

It's a little quieter since most of the kids are going toward the school. I lean over to put my other hand on her shoulder. She's sweating through the plain t-shirt she always wears.

"It is because..." she says a little shaky, "it's because Sulphur is yellow."

And doggone that girl stood up!

We are kinda wobbly, but hold on to each other. The breeze is blowing nice, and we enjoy that view. Then Miss Violet shouts, "Lenna! Jenna! Come on!"

"Look!" Jenna says.

And sure enough around our heads is that Cloudless Sulphur flopping-flying like flutterflies always do, trying to figure out which way it's going.

--END--

Lost

It's a couple of hours before dawn, and even if I didn't have a watch I'd know it. I've spent many misty mornings in these woods. I'm not hunting today, though, because my day got hijacked. It started with a stop for breakfast and drinks at Louder's Stop-N-Go around four a.m. When I walked in the door, Russell the morning clerk, frowned at me and pointed with his eyes to a shiny faced deputy in an overstuffed brown jacket.

Deputy Stanley asked straight up, "Hey, would you help us look for the missing Marten girl?"

"Hell, no. I'm going hunting," was my response. Russell, the deputy, and the two other people in the store looked at me like I'd been clubbing baby seals. "What? I don't even know what you are talking about," was my defense.

"She's that girl that's gone missing up near Tasselford."

I didn't know what he was talking about. A TV so old the glass is curved and a radio are my only electronic links to the world. I seldom use either. Last night I had flicked on the radio for the WSKY Sportsman's Report, and after hearing the forecast for a cloudy but rainless morning, I turned it off.

"I didn't hear about that," I said, and the explanation readjusted the faces of the men in the store.

The deputy explained that the girl had been hunting with her father yesterday afternoon but had gotten lost.

A hundred people tromping through the woods would pretty much eliminate any chance I might have to bag a deer so I decided to just go back home. Then big mouth Russell said, "Trip knows these woods as good as anyone. He'd be a good one to have out there looking."

I looked at Russell to blame him for getting me into this.

"Great," the deputy said and pulled up his clipboard, "What's your last name Trip? And what area would you be willing to help cover?"

"Trip Holmes," I said and seeing a chance to not let the day be a complete waste I added, "I'll go to the Sulfur Springs area." I had wanted to scout there anyway.

"You got a phone?"

I held up my flip phone. The silver paint has almost completely worn off the edges revealing the white plastic underneath, but it still works.

"Good. Just call 911 if you find anything."

I didn't bother to tell him there was no cell signal in the back hollers. I do have a handheld radio in the truck, and my buddy Steven has the mate.

It was still dark when I left Louder's. I headed up the mountain toward the pull-off for Sulfur Springs, and while I still had a cell signal I called Steven but got his voicemail. "Hey, I won't be hunting today. Got rooked into searching for some stupid kid who got lost in the woods. Turn your radio on. I may need to talk with you."

I turned on my Midland handheld radio and then the truck radio.

It crackled to life, "...already forming search parties. With temperatures expected to fall later today, timing is critical. [Engine revving] Jetway Auto is your one stop source for all your vehicle needs. Whether you need to trade in your old clunker or get an ATV for use on the farm..."

My headlights made the road in front of me look like a conveyer belt. The fog that hid the distance gave way as I passed through. I was hoping the Forestry Service had opened the gate to the Springs access road. If not, I would be hiking for at least a couple of miles. That's when I realized I hadn't gotten breakfast or coffee.

This day keeps getting better and better. Twenty minutes later I'm pulling up to the access road. A single metal pole painted yellow blocks the way—*better and better.*

I hunt with a 308, but I don't want to lug the extra ten pounds if it can't pay for its weight with meat. Neither do I want to leave it in the back window as temptation for a thief. I wrap it in a sweatshirt and tuck it behind the seat.

I grab the Midland, "Steven? This is Trip." No answer.

When it's dark like this, the woods seem vast and hollow. For all you know, the world has ended and what you see is the only thing left. It'd be a fine day for hunting—too bad I'm babysitting. That's the reason I didn't have kids. I don't really want to think about the other reasons I don't have kids. Let's just say, "She left," and leave it at that.

The old logging road is pretty level here and curves around to the right—hugging the steep slope. Also, to my right are the higher parts of the mountains to the northeast. The ground falls away on the left side of the dirt road and down to Sulfur Springs creek. Tasselford Road comes through the forest about five miles ahead.

Lots of tall trees and limestone bluffs between here and there. Early light is enough to make a difference between sky and branches but not enough to walk by so I click on my headlamp and move deeper into the woods.

The handheld hisses softly. I listen carefully for every other sound while trying to ignore the rustle produced by my own feet. Never mind that I've been in these woods a million times, it's always a little scary. A man can intrude into the wild, but he will always be the stranger here. I half regret my decision to leave the rifle. My pistol and knife are a poor match against a mountain lion or a bear.

As it often does my mind rolls back to that day.

"I just can't do it anymore, Trip," she said.

"You can't do what?"

"I can't go on pretending that you care about me."

"But I do care about you. Why would you say I don't care?" That last part came out harsh.

Marcie looked at me. Her brown eyes tinged pink from the tears, "You are never going to change."

"What? I've changed everything. I've dumped all my friends and all my booze. I don't hunt anymore..." the defenses rattled off like a train falling off a bridge. They were not true, but I couldn't stop spouting them out. I had cut back on the drinking and poker, but we still lived in the trailer, and I still worked for my uncle Kenny as a farm hand. And I looked most forward to being with her *after* I had been in the woods.

I couldn't confess the last part or deny it. "Look," I said, "I've been looking for another job. Even Kenny knows it. He's ok with it." How foolish to use Kenny as a witness. I didn't realize then that I had already lost her.

"Damnit Trip! I'm not a priority to you, and I never will be." Her look was painfully sharp, "You've been saying that for YEARS!"

I fell silent.

"I'm going to stay with my mother until I get my own place. I'll come get the rest of my stuff whenever you won't be here."

My pathetic response was, "Honey, don't do this. We can make it work."

"Yes, WE could have, but I've been the only part of the *we* working."

I was too beaten to reply, and she softened. "Look, Trip. I don't hate you. It's just there is no room for me and what I need in your life."

#

I shake my head to get it back to the present. The trail is starting to make its way down toward the creek. Fog has settled in the low spots. In the 1920s, the healing properties of the sulfur water and nearby caves created a draw. Hard to believe this place could be seen as a resort, but I suppose if it tastes bad, and it's uncomfortable, it's easy to believe it's good for you.

Big deer are in these woods in part because they are so hard to get to. My uncle has a saying, "The bigger the pain. The bigger the buck." Since I hunt mostly for food, I usually hunt doe rather than the trophies; but I've been thinking there could be a hoss in here for me.

The light is the faintest bit better now so I click off the headlamp and start my descent into the gray blanket. The moist air fills my lungs. My clothes are wicking the sweat away. Good gear makes a difference. I figure I've got another mile to go when I hear a loud crack. Instinctively, I lock down and reach for the revolver on my hip. I am motionless in a search for movement. Nothing small makes a crack that big. Now that I've stopped walking I can hear the creek, though the fog hides it from view.

"Trip. You there?" It's Steven on the radio, and I about piss myself.

I turn the volume down for another auditory survey. I hear nothing. I'll keep looking, but decide I may never know. And that's the way it is in the woods. Things happen that you can never know.

Steven comes through as I turn the volume back up, "—rip. Come in. Trip."

"Yeah, yeah I'm here. You 'bout gave me a heart attack."

"You ok?"

"Yeah, just looking for company."

"Oh. I got your message and wanted to touch base."

Steven and I have been friends since junior high. He had a wreck graduation night that left him paralyzed and maybe a little brain damaged. As friends peeled away, it seemed more important that I keep up with him. Now, he's married and has three kids. Unbelievable. He's in a wheelchair but freaking A still doin' it. The walkie-talkies are a way for him to go hunting with me. He keeps me posted on the weather, and it's a safety net for me I guess.

He continued, "I got your message about joining the search party. That's great!" He's always trying to pull me toward a more respectable life.

"Yeah, great."

"It can't be that bad. You're in the woods and doing a good deed."

"Yeah, on the second day of rifle season."

"Quit your grousing." When a guy in a wheelchair tells you to suck it up, ya probably ought to listen. He goes on, "Did you find anything?"

"No. I got some questions though. About this chick."

"Ok. Like what?"

"Like what the hell was she doing out here?"

Steven explained that the girl and her father were hunting the day before. Around dusk a couple of other hunters were making their way out of the woods. They spotted a dangling tree stand and went to investigate. At the bottom of the tree was the girl's unresponsive father. The hunters didn't see or know anything about the girl.

Steven went on, "They got the guy out to Tasselford Road and emergency teams took over. As they were trying to reach his next of kin they got ahold of his ex-wife, and that's when they discovered that the girl had been with him."

"How old is this kid?" I asked.

"Ten."

"Ten? Freakin' ten? What the heck?"

"Man, didn't you know?"

"I thought she was a teenager who wandered off drunk. Damn, that ain't good to be out here all night."

"Yeah. I've been listening to the news. Temp is going to drop later today."

I've made quite a number of things dead over the years, but I don't want to be the one to find the body of some kid. "Ok. Hopefully someone will find her." Mental images of a half-eaten carcass turn my empty stomach over. "Talk to you later Steven."

"Ok. Out."

If I turn off the trail to my left, I could get down the slope to the stream quicker, but I figure if the girl came across the road she might be smart enough to stay on it. I wish Marcie had stayed.

She did leave some things. She left Tuffy who never was hers anyway, but the old dog did miss her until the day he died. I've still got the hunting boots and the titanium flask she gave me. Why anybody would need a titanium flask was lost on me, but I suspect she got it because it was so small. "She always did try to cut back my drinking," I say, but fog cottons my words.

I pull out the flask from my left shirt pocket. It is small and round; I take a sip to distract myself from comparisons. I feel the cooling of the alcohol down my chest and fish out some jerky as I continue down the slope. I make my own jerky. That crap at the store ain't worth eating.

Marcie liked my deer jerky. She was no city slicker, and after I had given her some lessons she was no slouch with a gun either. I remember when she got her first trophy.

It was muzzleloader season, and I was her spotter. We'd been in the woods for hours, and she was whispering about leaving.

"I don't think we're going to get anything," she said under her breath. Her almond eyes were still scanning the forest. She had on her own jacket but had borrowed an insulated cap from me. Just her pointed nose and pretty face peeked out.

I hushed back, "Maybe just a little more. Sometimes the big bucks come out late."

She nodded seriously, and I loved her for the trust she placed in me. Then her big brown eyes got bigger—"Loook!" Just out of range, a good-sized buck was picking his way through the trees. He was passing through, not browsing, so she had to draw a bead on a moving target, and she did it! I was impressed, and I couldn't stop her excited chatter or my adoration. Honestly, that was the most beautiful I had ever seen her, and for a moment I forgot all about the deer. I still love her the same when I think about that.

As I've had to do many times, I blink the memory away, forcing attention to the here and now, but like the creek in the fog, memories are bubbling just out of view. I spend too much time looking back for what can't be seen. "God, I miss her," I say, but God already knows.

It's about five a.m. now and still an hour until dawn. I'm getting closer to the creek, and colder air greets me, but I'm warm from the walking. There are a lot of caves here—small pockets within the limestone bluffs. Some are thirty or forty feet deep but most are little more than overhangs. Between the leaf litter and the shade, nothing grows in them except some moss. The whole area has all kinds of appeal for deer: water, forage, and cover. A few more yards and I'll be in the bottom. I can't see the trail as it bends around another limestone outcropping. The path, if I remember right, sort of widens out and gets lost in the lowland. There are a few clearings ahead. This is prime hunting land, but you would want an ATV to haul one out.

I guess I do feel bad for this girl, and hope she ain't dead, but I have to say I'm most interested in spotting a good place for my tree stand. Besides, it would have taken her hours to walk this far into the woods. Hours she wouldn't have had because it would have been too dark.

As I say to myself, "She's not going to be here." I hear voices, indistinct and hushed, but the urgency is obvious. I wonder if it is another part of the search party. A trickle of fear runs down my back, and I wonder if it's some airhead growers.

Pot has never been my thing, and I don't care what they do, but runnin' up on someone cropping can be bad news. I could draw my pistol, but that sort of sets the wrong precedent. Instead, I take a few noisy steps forward and say, "Hey, anyone there?"

The voices drop, but I can hear footsteps approaching from around the rocks. I would rather them turn the corner before I do, so I slow down. A shadow of a man and a smaller person come into view. The fellow is wearing well-worn gear and has deep set eyes and a dark knit cap pulled over his skull. To his left is no doubt the missing girl. She's in an orange camo jacket with light colored hair spilling out from under her cap. Shadows conceal their faces, but the man is holding her wrist with his left hand. We both pull up to a slow stop about fifteen feet apart.

"Hey, guys," I say and hear the waver of fear in my voice.

"Hey there," comes from the man. He's physically fit and from the creases and grey stubble I figure he's in his fifties. The girl is looking at me with impossibly wide eyes but says nothing.

I wish I hadn't started the conversation. "I thought I might be able to bag a buck today," I say then ask, "You guys been hunting?" It's all wrong.

"Uh, yeah," the guy starts and seems to think better of it seeing how he's got no rifle and has a death grip on the girl's arm, His guard drops and he says, "This here is that missing girl. Found her up in them caves. She ain't talking. Must be shock, but I was taking her out."

"Oh. Great. I heard about that." I sound like somebody else. "You need any help?"

He ends our false conversation by saying, "No, I got it. We'll get going." Then he walks past me pulling the girl slightly behind. As he goes by he hears the hiss of my radio. Breath leaves my body as his eyes spot it on my left hip. I instinctively move my right hand toward the revolver.

"Why didn't you say you got a radio?" the man says sharply. "Let me have that thing, and we'll call it in. We won't have to walk so far."

My jacket is pushing back the heat from my body. "Oh, yeah, sure. I didn't think about that." I reach for the handset rather than my gun.

He says slowly, "Hand it to me if you don't mind."

They are up the slope from me now. I unclip the orange and black radio and reach up to hand it to him. He lets go of the girl and takes it with his left hand. For a moment I hope this is as it seems, but I know it's not. Then he raises his right hand and levels a gun it at my chest.

"Now, we are going to head out of here, and you go on hunting—without a rifle."

The weapon in his hand is exactly like my own, and my mind is racing around for clues on how he got it.

There is a blinding flash and deafening roar. My body spirals back and to the left from the impact. I fall face down like the earth is a magnet, and I am iron. Beyond the ringing in my ears, I hear the girl screaming. My chest feels impossibly warm.

#

It had taken me weeks to convince Marcie to move in with me. It finally happened in late October at the end of archery season. The trees still held some leaves, and the sunlight coated everything in butter.

As I pulled a box from the back of her car, I said, "Sorry about your job."

She just nodded, but I saw a tear.

"It's not right what they did," I offered.

The cardboard box was heavy with kitchen utensils. On the side in curly feminine marker was "Kitchen Stuff!" She faced me, and I figured she had probably struggled to load it. "I'm glad you are coming here, though. You know I am." I said.

"Yeah. I know. I'm excited, too. It's just, you know, I wanted to do things in the right order."

"Well, we'll get married soon. You'll have time to plan it all out."

"I guess."

Hefting the box I said, "Feels like you brought everything—including the kitchen sink!"

She laughed. And I adored her. I really did. I've never felt that kind of love for anyone. I wanted her to be happy, but I didn't know she wasn't going to budge on some things.

"You know I want a family, right?" she asked.

"Yeah, I know. I'm ok with it. Just give me a little time."

"Don't mess with me Trip Holmes. Married in the spring and kids not too far behind."

"Man, this box is getting heavy. I'm gonna take it in."

"I'm serious Trip."

"Yeah, I know."

She would use that same box when she moved out, but I've been stuck there between those two boxes.

I think I might have died but my head hurts like hell, and everywhere else I feel numb. My face is pressed into fallen oak leaves. The smell of the forest floor is what convinces me that I'm not dead. I hold my breath and listen. I hear nothing nor sense the faint pressure of someone nearby.

I can't tell how long I've been out. It's not as dark. Maybe thirty minutes until dawn. *Have I been here all night?* I roll over and can tell my clothes are not wet enough to have been here past dewfall. I look up the trail and grab for my cell phone in my chest pocket. I feel its shattered carcass and realize why I am alive. I pull out the heavily dented flask. The bullet is still lodged in the crevice of its own making.

Instead of a swig, I get up and start running. I feel like someone else has control of my legs, and a wicked gremlin has wound a cord around my neck in a serious effort to make my head explode. I need to move quickly, though, and quietly. The girl looked exhausted and maybe would be too tired to move very fast.

Her screams after the shot probably prevented the *coup de gras*. As I run, the weight of my own pistol pulls on my right hip. My mind tells me I'm an idiot for my prior confusion about how the man got my gun. He didn't. He just had his own.

I'm too preoccupied with how to not get shot again to come up with a plan. I'm just running with my eyes scanning the logging road. I see evidence of my passing and theirs. Then for the second time today Trip Holmes, mighty hunter and single fool gets surprised.

Bam! I hear the gunshot and flinch as if it were not already too late. I have no idea where the bullet hit but it did not hit me. Bam! Bam! The shots continue as I duck for cover down the slope off the right side of the trail.

"Boy, you should have stayed down. Now, I'm gonna kill you both!"

I only got a glimpse of him up around the left curving bend. He has ten yards of high ground on me. "Not good odds," my brain advises me. Then some idiot says, "Let the girl go!"

A laugh is his reply. I'm lying face down with my foot on a sapling to keep from sliding down the hill. I pull my gun. It looks better in my hand. My fear brain approves.

The girl is shouting something I can't understand. "Shut up!" the man growls at her, and I hear him coming my way. If he's holding onto her, I can't risk taking a shot, but she might mess with his aim. If he leaves her, she'll still be in danger should my shot miss. For better cover I scramble across the trail to the bank on the opposite side. The gun barks twice more, and my right thigh fails me from the impact.

Boggin-head comes around the bend dragging the girl beside him. His revolver is thrust out like his arm is in a straight cast.

Five feet away he sees me facing him down on my left side.

"Boy. You should have just left me alone."

"Not yet," I say and struggle to my feet. Blood is pouring down my leg in great warm pulses.

"You want to stand up for it? That's fine with me. It's the head this time though."

The click of an empty revolver is a distinctive sound, and his eyes and nostrils flare with fear as I raise my duplicate handgun. I've never killed a man before. Didn't know that I could, but it was easier than I thought.

The girl was a trooper. She helped me get a dressing on my leg. She even used the radio to call in help. Steven was serious, steady and efficient.

The rescue team should be here shortly. I've settled up with my back to the bank and the girl is beside me chattering about the cold night and how the creep was the first to find her and her dad after he fell. Instead of helping, he took her farther into the forest. I tell her that I think her dad is ok.

I'm trying to act normal, but I've lost a lot of blood. Dying seems a simple thing to do. To just let go. Wait. Accept. Tolerate. But I want something better for this tough little girl, and I'm doing my level best to not die on her. We have a deer jerky breakfast, and she eats a ton. I don't yet know her name, but she reminds me of Marcie.

--END--

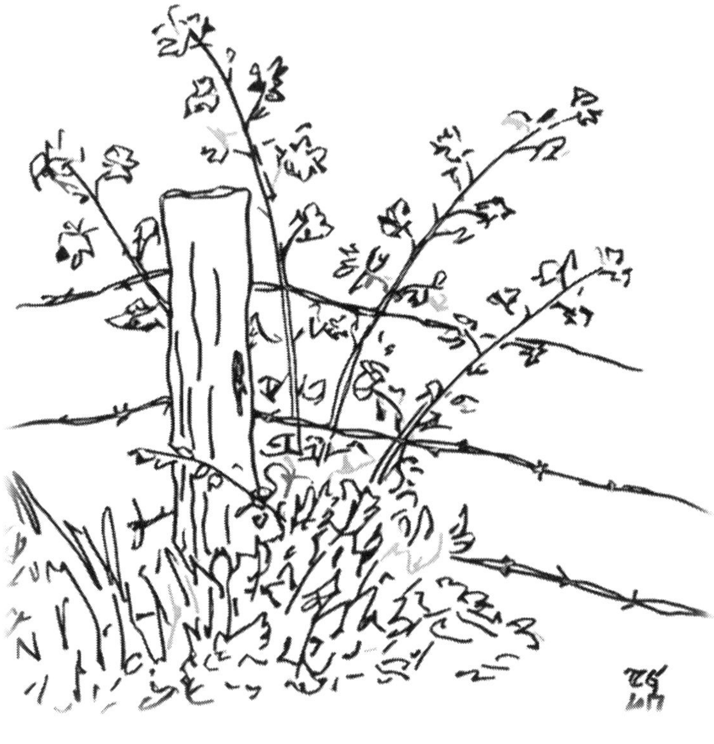

Blackberry

Maybell felt the heat pouring from her pores, but she couldn't stop running. Ahead of her was another rise, and she climbed it as fast as her eleven-year-old legs would carry her. The summer sun beat down on her dark skin as she ran up the chert road. To her right, wild blackberries mounded up trying to overtake a rusty barbwire fence. Like a rabbit, she kept looking for a passage big and dark enough to dart into. A mile back, her drunk and furious father was crawling into his battered old truck to come get her.

The bottoms of her pink flip flops did little to cushion the gravel, but her feet were tough and she was too scared to notice. Up the hill she went. Arms pumping. Lungs burning and heart pounding from exertion and fear. Back at the house, her father's movements were sloppy with alcohol. He had to pull the cab door closed twice to get it to latch. He didn't heed its advice.

Prater, Maybell's father, was an unfit parent by anyone's standard, but he still surpassed her mother, Angeline, by the simple fact that he was present. Prater and Angeline's relationship began when she was still a teenager. He was twelve years her senior. She used him for money, drugs and a way out of her momma's house. He used her for sex. Neither noticed when Angeline first became pregnant.

Between the highs and lows of their drug-centered life were brief moments in which they passed through normal. Those were times to interact with family and take note of things. That's when Angeline had told Prater simply, "I'm pregnant."

"So?" was his reply. There was no way for her to tell if his indifference was the slowly evaporating fog of last night's drinking or contempt.

"Well, what are you going to do about it?" Angeline asked.

"Nothing. What? What am I supposed to do? You're the one who got pregnant."

Anger sparked in Angeline. "What do you mean, 'I got pregnant!' You the one that's been screwing me!"

"Damn, but I didn't know you wasn't using something!"

The gravity of the situation sapped the energy for a big blowout and they fell silent.

Tentatively Prater suggested, "Go to the doctor. Make an appointment."

"I don't know about that."

"Well, me and you can't raise no baby."

"Abortion? You mean get an abortion?" She had considered the same thing, but his suggestion gave her a new angle to camouflage her own self-interests. From then on she could speak and act like she wanted Maybell, and he would be the "selfish wretch" who tried to abort her. The conflict became the core of the relationship. It worked for eight years; then Angeline followed the drugs and a new boyfriend-dealer up to Huntsville.

Framing himself as the victim of the abandonment, Prater was surprised by the level of sympathy it provoked. Between teachers and church folks, he got a few bills paid and an occasional babysitter, but that rally of support also made it impossible for him to bail out. His regular job and efforts to appear normal had been successful enough to make outsiders think he could be a father. If having your children cook, clean and get themselves dressed for school are the indicators of successful parenting, then Prater did a bang-up job.

He left every morning at 4:00 a.m. for the pallet mill. He bought whiskey on his way home and was drunk by 3:00 p.m. As he laid up in the living room or on the porch, Maybell took care of the house. She'd feed the cats, maybe sweep the floor, get supper together—usually heating up something from a can. Throughout the afternoon Prater would call from his seat for one thing or another. The recliner seemed to have a magnetic pull on alcohol. The more he drank, the less likely he was to move which was fine with Maybell.

His tottering around the house led to things for her to pick up or fix. There was not a table in the building with an unbroken leg. Occasionally, the stumblings led to a hard fall. If her mind had not already been trained to listen for every indication of movement, Maybell would surely have been able to know when Prater fell by the crescendo of swearing that rose angrily from the floor. That's what happened this morning. Being Saturday, the drinking started early and on the front porch.

"Maybell! Maybell!" Prater shouted. He sat upon an antique metal glider seat. Its smooth metal back was perforated with decorative punches. On the rolled top and arm rests, the paint had been replaced with smooth brown rust. Old towels and a tattered quilt served as cushions for him, and for the cats when he was elsewhere.

Maybell opened the creaky screen door and stepped into the wedge. "What?"

"Bring me a drink." Prater didn't have to explain. Maybell made her way back into the kitchen. Ancient gold Formica seemed downright contemporary next to the rounded white refrigerator. She opened the door looking for the blue plastic tea pitcher. Maybell's skinny arm prepared for the one gallon weight, but it was light. She pulled off the lid and looked inside. All it contained was the cool sweetened air she felt pass across her face. She set the jug on the counter and started to make tea.

Prater had dozed off, just for a moment, but the gap left him with the impression that it had been a lot longer. Angrily he hollered, "Where's my da'um tea?" Inside, the kettle was working its way toward a whistle, and Maybell didn't hear her father. The non-response ticked Prater from aggravation to anger.

"Where's. My. Damn. Tea?" he said slowly and loudly.

Not sure what he said, but knowing it reflected impatience about the tea Maybell answered, "I'm getting it, Daddy!"

It was Prater's turn to not hear clearly. His assessment was neither kind nor accurate. His impression of her distant words struck him as evasiveness. Rage flamed to life, and a pounding in his head heralded its arrival. It was a familiar but miserable parade with a vengeful victor out front and the defeated in tow.

Maybell could hear him cussing her. She couldn't decide if she should go explain that it was almost ready or wait until she could get it together and take it to him. She rushed to get the sugar in the jug, then poured in the steaming water—careful not to break the tea bags. With a gasp she grabbed a large plastic cup and packed ice in it as quickly as she could. "Just the right amount. Not too much," she urged herself.

She wasn't the only one moving. Rising with a full throat of fury, Prater pushed himself off his perch on the porch. The anger, alcohol and the rocking of the lounge made him totter. He had to stop swearing to gain his balance.

Maybell poured the hot tea. It fused the ice into a lacy block. She slapped it on the counter to break it up. Some of the hot-cold liquid splashed on her hand, and she turned and ran to the door holding it up like an Olympic torch. Prater and Maybell reached the front door at the same time. Neither saw the other. As he reached for the screen door with his right hand, she pushed it open with her left.

Startled, Prater jerked back and instinctively grabbed the wooden frame of the screen door. The unexpected opposition to her exit caused Maybell to throw the tea through the opening of the door and all over her father. In slow motion, Prater fell backward, tearing the weathered door apart under the force of his falling weight. Maybell saw the light of his wide-open eyes shift from surprise to fury before he hit the floor and tumbled off the porch.

The coming wrath was crystal clear, and although there was nowhere to go, Maybell started running for her life. She turned left out of the driveway kicking gravel up behind her and headed toward a gnarled old tree at the top of the rise. Born and raised in hard southern dirt, the oak's leathery leaves hung over dark shade; when Maybell arrived she immediately felt its protection from the sun and paused in the relief. But then an angry hopeless fear caught up with her and forced tears from her eyes. She looked back down toward her home and saw her dad's truck twist out of the drive. Dry terror clutched her throat, but when he turned the opposite direction it loosened enough for her to think.

Behind the oak, on the other side of the fence was a house not much different than her own—metal roof, deep porch and old. But it was different too. Instead of asphalt shingle siding, it had painted hardboard and was landscaped with flowers and shrubs. Maybell used the trunk of the tree to scale the fence. The barbs and brambles clawed for her, but she jumped free and made her way across the scraggly hayfield.

Maybell crept silently in the back door uncertain of her welcome but confident it was preferable to what was coming for her. A mismatched washer and dryer stood before her. Neatly painted wooden cabinets on the wall and eyelet curtains on the windows tried to disguise the room's former life as a porch. She quietly moved toward the opening to the kitchen. Peeking around the door frame she saw a large black woman working at the counter.

Without turning around the woman said, "Whatcha doing, honey?"

Maybell just stared, eyes wide to catch any reaction that would indicate danger.

"It's ok," the woman said. "You Prater Thompson's child? I remember you from Vacation Bible School."

The woman turned slowly toward Maybell. She wore a ruffled apron around her ample waist. She had large hands and a smooth face. Maybell continued to stare like a cat watching a stranger pass by.

Blackberry

"Well, you can sit down. I'm making some pies for the bake sale. Maybe you would like some—they're all blackberry, though." She turned back to her work on the counter.

Maybell took a quick step into the kitchen and immediately sat down in a straight-backed chair under the light switch. She had not noticed at first, but now the whole room was filled with the buttery sweet aroma of fresh baked pies. She could see the golden brown crusts cresting over the aluminum pans on the countertop. Her mouth started to water and along came a distant memory of hot pie filling burning her tongue. She pressed her tongue to the roof of her mouth and squeezed out the saliva with remembered pain.

"We're having a fundraiser at church, and I was gonna take these down to sell."

Maybell looked around the room. A large wooden table sat in the middle with counters and cabinets on three sides. Sunlight provided most of the light. Maybell's stomach purred.

"I'm Doris Waters. What is your name, honey? Mabel?" Mrs. Waters mused.

"Maybell."

"Ok, Maybell. I think you need to help me taste test these pies."

Maybell nodded, but a loud knock on the front door froze her solid.

Mrs. Waters moved effortlessly toward the door wiping her hands down her apron. Maybell wanted to shout out "No! No! Don't go to the door!" but only a squeak came out. She couldn't see the door from where she sat, but instinct located the threat. When she regained control of her body, Maybell crept to the opening between the kitchen and living room. She could see Mrs. Waters standing inside the open front door. From the shadow Maybell could tell someone was standing opposite her—just outside.

"Well, son, you don't need to worry about that," the old woman said.

Maybell couldn't hear the other side of the conversation but could tell it was her father.

Mrs. Water's laughed, "No, no that won't be necessary. I'll just keep her here for a little while until things settle down. Ok?" It wasn't really a question, but the muttered response was not in agreement.

"Now, let me tell you something, Mister Thompson. If you don't remove your drunk ass from off my front porch, I'm going to call the Sheriff and have you arrested." Then, suddenly, Mrs. Waters turned into the house and shouted, "Harold? Harold can you come here, please?"

The shadow moved off the porch grumbling. Mrs. Waters closed the door. Maybell stood up and marveled at the woman. As if nothing extraordinary had just happened, Mrs. Waters asked, "Now, where were we? Oh, yes! About to have some pie!"

"That was your father, honey," she said as she walked past Maybell on her way to the kitchen. "He's gonna let you stay here for a while. I told him my grandkids hadn't been around much this summer, and I was kind of needing some company of children."

Maybell found her a place at the table while Mrs. Waters poured a glass of milk and put a piece of pie in front of her. The pie filling was warm but not hot. The crust was perfectly crumbly. The berries had a sour edge, and Maybell's mouth watered again as she dug into it.

"You know what makes blackberries sweet, child?" the old woman asked.

"Nu uh."

"'No, ma'am.' Maybell. A young lady says 'No, ma'am.'"

Maybell wiped her mouth with the back of her hand. "No ma'am."

"Blackberries grow in tough places. Scrub land where it's hot and dry and that hard living makes them either hard and bitter or plump and sweet. I reckon the berry has to decide."

"Of course a little sugar in the mix helps them too!" Mrs. Waters laughed.

Maybell looked down the hallway listening. Except for the whirring of the ceiling fan the house was quite. "Who's Harold?" Maybell asked.

"Why that's my cat, honey."

--END--

Clouds

"How do you know your parents don't love you?" the therapist probed Kevin's observation.

"Because they don't ever ask where I'm going. And they don't ever tell me 'no,'" Kevin said.

The therapist couldn't disagree.

Thin, tall and with short hair, Kevin's clean looks matched his thinking and he was a straight-A student when he wanted to be. As he left the office, he pulled out his phone to text his buddy, Rick. They had plans to smoke later.

With many variables beyond their control, Kevin and Rick kept arrangements fluid. Their activities were dependent on other things falling into place like access to transportation, when parents would get home, if chores were done.... Plans, therefore, were more like placeholders while discussions about what they could do and would do mixed reality and fantasy to the point of indistinction. That open-endedness left room for the unexpected, including disaster.

"Hey," Kevin texted.

"What up," Rick texted back.

"We still on?"

"O Yeah!"

Thick gray clouds had given way to thin ones high in the sky. The kind that fuzz out the sun and diffuse its light. Warm and breezy. It was a lovely day.

Rick was already at the courthouse square when Kevin arrived in his small blue truck. With its faded paint and mismatched wheels, Kevin didn't have much pride in his ride. Downtown was little more than a ring of small shops, lawyers' offices and a movie theater—the Oldham. Everything except the theater was closed by 6:00, so Kevin had his choice of parking places.

Rick was seated on a bench outside of the courthouse. Suitably torn jeans and a slightly oversized leather jacket helped convey the persona Rick wanted for himself. He acted like he didn't see Kevin because the presence of the truck made the lack of his own transportation painfully obvious.

"Hey, man," Kevin said.

"Hey, what up—you should have seen them girls just over here. Melissa Kell is H.O.T.!"

"You're an idiot," Kevin chided. "She'll freaking give you AIDS."

"She's so hot she'd kill the virus," Rick countered.

They had been friends since grade school when it was easier to find things in common and less important what others thought about you. Kevin was pretty sure Rick's dad was an alcoholic and that Rick's home life was even more chaotic than his own. The shared sense of alienation from their parents had deepened their friendship as they got older.

Kevin looked across the square at a family of three entering the movies. He pictured the scene at his own home: Dad sitting at his desk doing bills or reading, and Mom and his sister Carrie chatting and getting dinner ready together.

"I got some good stuff," Rick said excitedly and patted his chest pocket. Kevin could see the anticipation on his friend's freckled face. "It's gonna be gooooood!"

Kevin noted a key difference between them. He mused to himself that Rick liked the idea of being delinquent more than he liked getting high. Kevin rarely gave any thought to the illicit nature of pot smoking; he used the drug to distract himself from nebulous pain.

Together the two walked to the theater. Rick was talking about a fist fight at school. Kevin was comparing the two movies being shown. One was a family friendly story about a spunky dog. The other was an action movie demonstrating various ways combatants might kill each other in the future.

Their classmate, Hillary, was running the ticket booth. It was an old-fashioned glass box with a metallic circular grill in the window and a steel lined opening for the cash and tickets to slip through. She smiled brightly at Kevin. Rick smiled brightly at her.

Grades might have come easy for Kevin, but girls were a different matter. The dull ones couldn't hold his interest, the pretty ones required too much investment, and the emotional ones moved toward him like he was a low powered tractor beam. His disinterest was magnetic. If he had wanted to take it, the player path was laid out for him, but he didn't have any desire to ride out the twists and turns of a high school relationship.

The movie was a mindless series of explosions, expletives and contrived drama. Kevin imagined that aliens observing the theater might think the measured doses of flash and fury on screen could be a source of nutrition to the viewer—a visual and auditory cafeteria for the mind. *We should have hit it before the movie,* Kevin thought.

#

After the film Rick was anxious to get to the pot. So, when Kevin got penned in the popcorn perfumed lobby by a trio of emo classmates, Rick motioned that he would be out back. Behind the theater there was an alcove, hidden from the street, where two buildings came together. A set of long unused concrete steps led down to a basement door fastened tight with steel bars. Last year's leaves sprinkled the steps and covered the landing at the door. It was a perfect spot for them to burn a few.

Rick made his way under the steel fire escape stairs that clung on rusty bolts to the flat brick wall. It was dark and damp. His shoes got wet as he walked through the patchy unmown grass. His mind bounced back and forth between the creepy surroundings and the anticipation of the new weed.

His brother's friend had set him up with "a little something special." Rick could have known the pot was laced with another drug, but he didn't want to know. As he pulled out the blunt, he thought of the difference between his willingness to skip around on facts and Kevin's inability to suspend his handles on reality. Should they have to cross a stream, he thought, he would have leapt from rock to log to rock carelessly getting his feet wet. Kevin would have dammed and drained the channel then waited a week for it to dry up. Rick laughed out loud at the thought of Kevin being so patient. He laughed even harder when he realized his feet were actually wet.

#

The brightly lit lobby of the theater was crowded with all kinds of people, but the teenagers created the most buzz. Kevin was cornered by a semi-circle of girls with blacked out eyes, pale skin and dark clothes. When another classmate approached the group, Kevin took the chance to say he had to go. He could not have known Rick would be dead by the time he got to him.

Rick stood at the bottom of the stairwell. He could feel the cool moisture of the concrete around him. It smelled of mold and decaying leaves. Fungal dampness felt like it was pushing into his lungs and skin. He was inclined to wait until Kevin arrived but decided to take a hit or two. The first puff was a small one just to get it lit, but on the second take Rick inhaled deeply and had a physiological reaction to the stimulant in the weed. He didn't even exhale—the vapors were forced out of his mouth when his body slumped to the ground.

Following almost exactly the same steps Rick traveled, Kevin came around the back of the buildings. There was just enough light to make out the puff of smoke above the stairwell. "That dweeb didn't wait for me," Kevin thought. Radio silence was the rule when smoking weed behind the theater. The line of sight might be blocked from the street, but sound travels freely around corners.

When Kevin arrived at the top of the stairs, it took a moment for his mind to recognize what he was seeing. He expected to see Rick standing by the forsaken door smirking at him with a tiny orange glow lighting up his face. Instead, he saw a dark lump crumpled in the corner. Rick could have passed for a black plastic garbage bag except for the sock-covered ankle laying awkwardly in the leaves. In the murky darkness it looked to Kevin like the denim leg of Rick's pants was the open mouth of a toothless creature swallowing the last bit of his friend.

"Rick!" Kevin rushed down the steps. "Rick!" He shook his friend by the shoulders. He moved his hands to the sides of Rick's clammy face. "Rick! Look at me!" Kevin put his head against Rick's chest. There was no breathing, and he couldn't hear a heartbeat. Until now his own heart had done its job imperceptibly, but now it lurched forward with the realization his friend was dead.

As he pulled Rick's legs out from underneath him, Kevin cradled his rag doll head until he was flat on his back. Kevin took a deep breath and shouted, "Help! Somebody help me!" He took another deep breath and blew hard into his friend's mouth. He noticed the bitter aftertaste of smoke and something sickly sweet. Again he forced air into Rick's lifeless body. When he sensed Rick's chest rise, a little hope rose in Kevin. Then he saw the movement was only the result of his own actions. His mind raced to remember how to do CPR. Between breaths he shouted for help and executed panicked awkward compressions on his friend.

Time is not the same around death. It took five minutes before someone followed Kevin's cries for help around the building, but Kevin felt like he would be there forever. His muscles and lungs were burning, still he kept going until the paramedics arrived.

Flashlights—super-blue bright beams—seemed to come from nowhere. They floated overhead dividing the stairwell into luminous surfaces and deep shadow. Grown men were shouting and jostling in the tight space. It was a blur to Kevin. When the first responder said, "I got him, kid," and slapped a hand-held respirator over Rick's mouth, fearful relief moved Kevin to tears.

He cried for Rick and for the crappy life he had lived. He cried that he had been part of the wasting of it, but he cried the most when Rick began to sputter and cough and the paramedic said, "He's breathing!"

Four hours later Kevin was sitting alone in the ER lobby. From his seat near the window, he had seen Rick's parents park in the loading zone and scurry in the front doors of the hospital. His mom had to help steady his intoxicated father who cussed at her when the automated doors were slow to open.

A nurse offered Kevin something to drink. He declined. The TV was on a cable news station but nobody was watching.

A little after 1:00 a.m., the ER doctor came out to give Kevin a report, "He got ahold of some bad stuff, and it triggered a cardiac arrest. The drug test came back positive for cocaine and methamphetamine, but we sent off to Nashville for the full toxicology report."

"He's going to be ok?" Kevin asked.

"Yeah, I think he will be fine. We're going to keep him overnight and see what kind of other help he needs."

Visible relief washed over Kevin, "Thanks. Thanks for letting me know."

"You know you saved his life, don't you?"

"Huh?"

"If you hadn't been there, he would have died. You restarted his heart for him," she said. Kevin looked at the doctor like she spoke in a foreign tongue.

"Well, I need to get back in here. Do you need a phone or a ride or anything?" the doctor asked.

Kevin held up his phone. The doctor turned and went back inside. The doors closed silently behind her.

It took Kevin twenty minutes to walk back to his truck on the square. It was the second time that evening he had broken a sweat, and he was ready for a shower. When he pulled up in his driveway at home, the moonlight was trying to find the ground through the still leafless trees. He made his way into the side door and into the shower.

High above and unobserved, bright clouds moved silently across the sky, going nowhere.

--END--

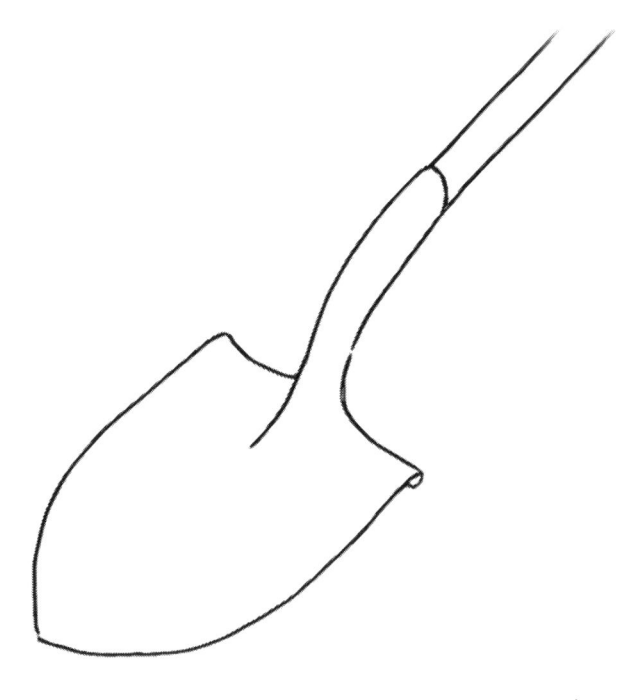

Bones

Leafless sycamore trees clutched at the gray winter sky like fingers of a skeletal hand. Leonard Mattingly looked across the field through the unwashed window of his truck. The vehicle was thirty years old, and Leonard was more than twice that. Both showed the wear of age; and the rust and dents of work and rowdy play.

"Damn cold," Leonard said as he rattled out of the cab. The door squeaked in protest. Beyond the field and across the creek was an even colder spot. He had come to remember and to forget. The icy wind quietly passed through the white-barked trees and over the fallow ground. His boots crunched the frozen ground as he made his way toward the creek and what lay beyond.

#

Leonard first met Lila when she came to the co-op on an errand for Mrs. Tidwell. He had not worked there long. Too much drinking, and the associated quarrels, had cost him his job as one of Cecil McGovern's farm hands. Lila came in wearing a red and white dress with a matching scarf in her hair. With her seventeen-year-old zest for life, Lila brought her own light into the dusty store. She wanted all eyes on her, and the world complied.

Stumbling from behind the counter, wiping his hands on the front of his jeans, Leonard asked, "What can I do for ya, Miss?"

Lila's eyebrow arched at the attention. "Oh, I'm here for Mrs. Tidwell. Says she needs some iron for her hydrangeas. Do you sell that here?"

Leonard instinctively recognized the selection of her intense and theatrically red lipstick as both an appeal for interest and an indication of her inexperience with makeup. With an untouching hand he ushered her in front of him and maneuvered her to the soil supplement in the most indirect way possible. His thoughts were lustful and possessive but he knew anything overtly sexual could cause her to bolt. *No, this will be a bit of a slow walk*, he said to himself. He tried to discern her figure under the colorful dress.

"But once I'm in, I'll be in," he said under his breath. "What sir?" she asked.

"Oh, I was just saying to myself how pretty you are...Miss?"

Blushing Lila said, "Lila. My name's Lila."

"Yes, you sure are pretty, Miss Lila."

Nodding down at a barrel with white and yellow stripes Leonard said, "This here is what you're looking for." When she smiled in agreement, white teeth behind painted lips, he scooped out five pounds into a heavy paper sack.

Lila charged the purchase to Mrs. Tidwell's account and said in her most grownup voice, "Thank you, sir."

When she turned to leave, Leonard called out, "Now, you come back here if there is anything else you need. We got just about anything you could ever want." Lila smiled and, with a flourish of her ponytail, left the store. Before dust, oil and hardware could drown out the fading scent of her perfume, Leonard was already making plans to work her need for attention to his advantage.

Soon they were seeing each other though they told no one of their relationship. He was seven years her senior, and she was still in high school. Mrs. Tidwell provided unwitting cover for their rendezvous. Lila would lie to her parents that Mrs. Tidwell had asked her to come help with something, and they would give permission and the pair would sneak off to deserted places.

She was resistant at first to his sexual advances but to preserve his affection she had slowly conceded ground to his taunts and demands. A mix of extended compliments on her beauty, petitions to meet his "needs as a man," and chiding her reservations as childish, eventually proved sufficient. Two months later, Lila and Leonard lay on their backs in the bed of his truck. Hay and a tattered quilt provided cushion. "Cecil McGovern is a prick," Leonard was complaining.

"Don't say that. He's a nice enough man."

"He's a pompous, self-righteous prick."

Lila had already learned to shift away from disagreements and asked, "What are we going to do tomorrow?"

He didn't follow her lead.

"That ass fired me for no good reason. Been working there since I got out of school, and he just gets all pissy because I wouldn't stop drinking. Damn! I'm old enough to drink if I want!"

Leaving her hand on his chest, Lila sat up and looked down at him. Her eyes were troubled. His lips were drawn tight over his teeth. "Oh, Lenny, let's go do something fun," she pleaded.

"You wanna drink?" Leonard asked—probing at the next boundary.

"No. You know I don't want to drink any," Lila protested.

"Damn, girl, you sure are prissy!" Leonard laughed at her.

#

Leonard focused on the walking instead of the destination. It was almost noon, but it wouldn't be getting any warmer. His shadow went on before him like a well-trained dog scampering over the furrows but staying near. Chinese privet formed its tattered but evergreen hedge under the creekside trees. He looked for an opening. A dark space to his right proved to be an adequate passage through the volunteer hedge. Leonard wondered who had worn the path.

As he made his way through the undergrowth, it became clear the path served as access to a swimming hole. An old anger rose within him like a flame with no heat. When he had worked for Cecil, the old farmer would never allow him and his friends to dam up the creek for a swimming hole. But now a sturdy wall of stacked stones and slick leaves formed a leaky barrier to the water's flow. By itself it wouldn't have been sufficient, but the rocks were stacked upon a creek-bed shelf just where the banks pinched together. The pool was nothing spectacular, but more than enough to get wet.

#

"Hey, you boys move them logs out of the way! I don't want you damming up my creek!" Cecil shouted down at his farm hands splashing in the water.

Leonard said back, "Ah, it ain't doing no harm. We was just making the hole a little deeper."

"I don't care what you were doing. I ain't gonna have it."

Leonard glowered at him. Looking down from the steep bank Cecil demanded, "I ain't gonna tell you again. Tear it down." The old man walked off.

"Tear it down, Leonard. I ain't gonna stand fer it!" one of Leonard's coworkers teased. The others joined in the ribbing.

"Why, ever since I got off the ark with Noah, I don't like puddles of water."

"Yep, and that Leonard is always damming things up."

"Yup, just last week he dammed up the hydraulics on my big tractor."

The taunts fueled Leonard's hatred. Grins faded when Leonard finally snarled, "I'm gonna kill that somebitch."

#

To her dismay Lila realized too late that Leonard was on his well-rehearsed rant against his former boss. "That old codger was just a Bible thumpin' know-it-all. Won't even let us build a little swimmin' hole to cool off in!"

Leonard got up from the bed of the truck and slammed his fist into his hand, swearing at a man not even present. Lila moved to Leonard's side to soothe him. Gently her fingers lighted on his arm.

He snapped his arm away and screamed in her face, "I'm going to kill that man!" She smelled the alcohol on his breath and her heart sank.

"Don't say that—"

"Don't say what? Don't say I'm going to kill Cecil McGovern?" His face contorted into a blood-red mask. "I'm going to kill Cecil McGovern! Hear me? I'm gonna kill Cecil McGovern, and he's got it coming to him for what all he done to me!"

Lila said the last words of her young life. "He wasn't that bad to you."

Strengthened by well rehearsed fury, Leonard viciously struck her. His work-hardened fist slammed into Lila's face, and she fell to the ground. He had felt something break, but it was not any of the bones in his hand. He stood over her crumpled body still furious. Her legs were bent awkwardly beneath her. Any motion, cries or resistance would have brought more blows, but there was none. She didn't move. The only movement was a trickle of blood falling from her mouth onto the dusty soil. Leonard realized he had killed her.

He didn't feel sad or afraid. He just stopped feeling enraged. He stared at her for a long time as his mind came to terms with what he was seeing. The loud squawk of a crow pulled him from the eddies in his mind, and Leonard immediately began to think of how to dispose of her. Tools, machinery, and locations swarmed his mind. He pulled a tattered brown tarp from his truck. After wrapping her in it, he stuffed her under the toolbox in the bed. He then pushed the spare tire and truck-bed litter of hay, rags, and bottles up as camouflage.

He decided to drive around town and buy gas and cigarettes to form some alibi. To soothe his nerves and shade the stark reality of his situation, he made another stop soon after dark for beer. He almost lost his composure though when the clerk at the package store asked, "You up to no good?"

Leonard stared coldly at the young man.

"Or up to a good time?" the clerk grinned with a nod to Leonard's case of beer.

"Oh. Yeah." Leonard said. A vision of Lila's foot jutting out from under the trash in his truck bed intruded into his mind. Instinctively, his eyes turned toward his vehicle parked just outside the doors to the store. A faulty fluorescent light made it appear like his headlights were faintly blinking at him.

Seeing his intense stare the chatty clerk asked, "What? The cops after you already? You *are* planning a good time." Leonard grimaced as if swallowing something bitter, and the clerk grew concerned, "Take it easy, man."

Leonard wrenched his eyes away from the truck, knowing that his behavior looked odd to the young man. Sweat cooled his brow. "Yeah. Uh. I just thought somebody was messing with my truck."

"Man! Seriously? Want me to go check it out? Been some guys thieving around here. My boss says he'd give me a hundred bucks if I catch 'em!" The clerk was already moving around the counter. Leonard would have grabbed his arm, but his own were full of canned beer. The clerk slipped by and out the door, saying, "Just sit that on the counter. I'm gonna go take a look."

After a flash of fear, Leonard put the beer down and decided he was going to have to kill at least one more person. The young man moved past the awning lights and was lost in the shadows and reflections of the windows. Leonard stepped outside as the clerk started back to the building. The clerk put his right hand on the bed of Leonard's truck and paused. He said, "I didn't see nobody. Must have run off."

Leonard visualized grabbing him by the shoulders and slamming him face first into the pavement. The tire iron in the bed would do the rest.

"You say they were messing with your truck?" the clerk asked, peering over into the bed. Leonard stepped toward him. The clerk's prattle continued, "I reckon they got away. Need to check you out, I guess." When the young man turned toward the store, he bumped into Leonard. Startled, he said, "Man! I didn't see you there."

"It's all right," Leonard said. The clerk hadn't noticed a thing. "Can I get my beer?"

Leonard drank a few and drove around some more. He rolled past the deserted co-op, looped the square and found himself going by Lila's home. Warm light streamed through the windows. Country music played on his radio, but Leonard didn't notice. Lila's body right behind his back brought a paradoxical sense of confidence. A couple of hours after midnight, he drove past Cecil McGovern's tobacco barn. He turned off his headlights and tried to minimize the brake lights, but it wouldn't have mattered anyway. Even the earliest risers wouldn't be up for a few more hours. He made his way through two gates. The second was a barbwire gate with three strands tied to a fixed post on one side and a moveable post on the other. As he pulled the post free from the wire loop, it cut a gash across the back of his hand. It began to bleed, but Leonard didn't notice until the steering wheel began to feel sticky.

Under starlight, he drove to Cecil's back field burn-pile. He knew it would have some brush and trash already there, but the big burn would come in late fall when the fence rows got cleared. The tall grass gently tapped the truck as it crept up to the mound of limbs. He turned on the headlights. The green eyes of a small animal flashed at him from within the brush pile then disappeared.

His plan was to bury Lila under the brush and use the ashes to cover the digging. With his shovel, Leonard created an open space near the center and raked back the charcoal and ashes. He began to dig. The exertion opened up the wound on his hand and, like the steering wheel, the ash handle started to feel sticky. The dampness of the night air fell on him as he worked. The blood gave way to sweat, and forty minutes later, he took a break. The hole was nearing four feet deep and the sides were fairly vertical. With the brush and the hole to his right and the truck behind him, he looked out toward the creek. It was just a dark mass of trees. It startled him to see the green eyes again.

"What the hell are you?" Leonard croaked. He was surprised by the rasp in his own voice. Crickets chirped their background noise, but the eyes didn't answer. He resumed digging. The excavated dirt formed a bigger mound than he expected.

"Might be too much on top. Just have to toss the extra into the field," he decided.

The lights of the truck suddenly dimmed, and the thought of the vehicle failing to start sent his heavy beating heart to a harsh thudding. He started the engine and the beams brightened. Peering into the creek-side thicket, he saw the green eyes a third time. They were low and nearer now to the burn area. A faint silver outline revealed fur.

Leonard stepped out of the truck, and the fox turned away silently. Leonard had another intrusive thought—*what if some animal digs up the body?* "Damn," Leonard said and trudged back to the hole. He made it a foot and a half deeper before his strength started to fail. "That's enough," he said.

He went to the back of the truck and lowered the tailgate. The red glow of the taillights made his arms appear very dark. He climbed in and pulled the spare tire away and brushed aside some of the camouflaging trash. He grabbed the tarp and pulled Lila out of the truck. She felt like an extra heavy bag of feed.

He carried her to the impromptu grave and dumped her face down into the cavity. He had to lie on his stomach and reach down to get her body to lie flat and to tuck the loose tarp ends under her. Shoveling in the dirt went more quickly than the digging. Two or three times he stopped to pack the earth with his feet. He allowed a mound of about a foot to account for some settling and covered it all with the old ashes. Finally, he pried up one of the larger logs to rest across the grave.

The shovel rattle-scraped across the truck bed, and he quietly closed the tailgate. He sat in the cab looking at the brush pile for a moment. He knew it would look more disturbed in the daylight, but he was counting on the fact that, except for a possible final hay cutting, the field would be unvisited for months. The fox walked back into the beams of the headlamps. Its eyes still shining green with reflected light.

"Just me and you know," Leonard said. "I'll keep my mouth shut, and you do the same."

He showed up for work on time the next day and every day for months. The newspaper headlines grew in size and intensity before fading back to nothing.

"Local Girl Missing" became "Foul Play Suspected in Disappearance" and finally, "Still No Answers for Grieving Family."

#

The sixty-something-year-old Leonard crossed the creek using the makeshift dam. Coming out of the creek brush into the opposite field, Leonard turned his head away from the grave. Straight ahead and over the rise was the last gate where he cut his hand those many years ago. Far off to the right was old man Cecil (now dead man Cecil's) house. "Not by my doing," Leonard said.

Slowly, he turned his gaze left and toward the cold spot. The burn pile was still there. A couple of small half-burned tree limbs ringed the dark earth like black worms crawling out of the ground.

He had never told anyone about what happened. Years before, he thought about sending an anonymous letter to Lila's parents, but the idea was shut out after its moment of cognition. Nobody knew, and it was going to remain that way.

He walked through the frozen field grass to the burn pile. Staring over the ashes, he spoke into the wind, "I don't know why I'm here. I guess part of me feels bad for what happened to you. It's been wearin' on me a lot, though." Leonard stood just inside the blackened ring while the cold bit into his leathery face and ears. "I've never told no one. Sorry about your parents' divorce—" Then he cut himself off, "You're crazy, old man." His eyes watered from the cold.

He took a deep breath and began again, "Like I said, I can't say why I'm here. Maybe just to say I done it.

Maybe just to say it out loud. So, now Miss, I want you to let me go. You don't know no better, and I've had all these years to carry this alone. So let me go, Lila. You owe me that much. Let me go." That bit of rising resentment helped him turn away. Inadvertently, his boot kicked over a thick lump of ashen earth. Looking down, he recognized the smooth bone of a human skull.

Leonard's mind began to reel like a small boat atop stormy water. "I buried her; I know I did. And deep too!" he stumbled away. Eyes wide with a dawning awareness, he turned back to face the cold spot.

"You couldn't have. You was dead. You couldn't have come out!" Images of Lila struggling to disinter herself flashed through his mind like reflectors on a passing train. Clawing. Struggling. Then dying there half buried.

"No!"

Leonard lurched away from the grave and from the thoughts he would not allow himself to consider. He pushed through the privet underbrush as it scratched at his face. Slow and teetering, he moved across the rock dam back the way he had come. Halfway across, he saw a fox sitting on the far side of his bridge to the truck. Startled, Leonard put out his arms to balance himself and teetered to a stop. The fox did not move. Its large dark eyes regarded him dispassionately.

"Go on!" Leonard shouted.

The fox did not flinch. "Go on! God damn you!" he roared and threw up his arms to scare beast and the unburied memories away. It was just enough motion and distraction for Leonard to lose his footing. He plunged into the deep cold water.

#

Sheriff Pat Lawrence was taking a report from his greenest deputy, Nick Wilson. "Damd'est thing I've ever seen." Wilson was saying. *Stick around,* the Sheriff thought. "This guy over here frozen solid on the creek bank is one Leonard Mattingly. Sixty-three-year old local."

"Yeah, I know him. Drinker, but he knew enough to toss 'em back at home."

"Seems that he fell in the crick before crawling out to die of hyperthermia."

"Hy-*po*-thermia Wilson. Hypothermia. Which I'm getting right now listening to you—So tell me why I'm out here looking after a drunk who froze his fool ass off."

"Well, sir. We thought it was just that until we crossed into McGovern's field—that's his field on the other side—"

"I know, son. I know whose damn field it is."

"Well, anyway we were trying to trace his steps and turns out there is a human skull over there."

"Hmmm," the Sherriff said slowly, "bones."

--END--

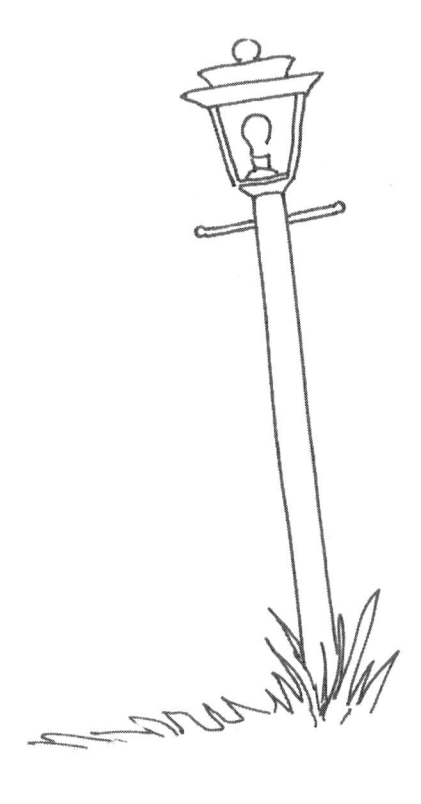

Post

My wife bought some new shampoo. Now I smell like fruit. The shaving cream helps. My thinning hair indicates there is some testosterone in there, but I'm not feeling it today. "Daddy! Daddy!" I hear my eight-year-old daughter call out as she tromps my way. "I need yooouu to fix my backpaaaaack!"

There is a rip at the starting end of the zipper. She needs a new one, but you put off what you can. I turn the bag inside out and use a stapler to mend it. "It ain't perfect, but at least it works," I tell her.

"Thank you, daddeee!" Only a child can make everything sound exciting.

At the end of our drive, a slightly leaning lamp post in the yard points toward my job where there will be more problems to fix. It used to stress me out, but I've learned to just do what's in front of me. The boss still tries, like now, to make me stress like him. "James," he says, "line seven is behind, and I think the belt is slipping."

That's all I need to know, but he keeps talking, "If we don't get that running right today then second shift is going to start off on the wrong foot, and we are going to get even further behind...."

He goes on for some time listing all the things eating at him. I want to tell him to shut up since yapping about something you can't or aren't going to do anything about is just unnecessary aggravation. Talking about problems doesn't make *me* feel any better, but if I'll let my wife air it out, it seems to help her move on. I don't want to talk about things though. Just give me what I got to do and get out of the way. I interrupt my boss, "Ok. I'll get right on it." He's a little miffed I didn't get infected with his tension, but he just looks constipated and turns away.

At lunch, my buddy, Frank also wants to talk to me. He thinks his teen daughter is pregnant. My older daughter Holly is the same age. I don't even want to consider her doing the same thing.

"She broke down last night. Melody confronted her and she just started crying," Frank tells me.

"So what did she say?"

"She didn't really say, but after it was over Melody said she was going to take her to the doctor tomorrow—today."

"Well, then you'll know."

"But I won't know if I should beat the crap out of that boy!"

I know Frank won't assault anyone. He's just pissed. And he doesn't need me to tell him the part his daughter had in it. I just say, "I'd want to do that too. What time is the appointment?"

"I don't know. Ten I think."

"They gonna call you?"

"Lord, I hope not. Not at work."

"Yeah, better just to wait until you can deal with it. What do you have for lunch?"

"Brisket."

"Lucky dog."

"Yeah, I know."

After work, I go by the school to pick up Holly from volleyball practice. She gets in and starts talking, but after about the third illogical leap in subject I lose track of whatever she's talking about. I don't know half the kids she's chattering about either, but if I interrupt it takes even longer to get the stories out. I just listen...and thank God she's not pregnant.

When I get home, I make my son help me with the leaning lamp post in the front yard. We've only got a couple of hours of daylight left. I have to tear him off the game console.

"Grab that bag of concrete," I tell him. He's fifteen and stouter than I was at that age.

"I don't want to do this," he says, even though he knows it won't make a difference.

The lamp post was installed by a previous owner and for the last year or more it's been leaning. I see it every day as a reminder of a long list of things I need to get done. Every once in a while, my wife nags me about it. It's like a script.

"When do you think you will be able to fix that lamp post?" she says.

"I don't know."

"Well, are you going to take care of it or not?"

"I didn't say I wasn't going to do it. I said I didn't know WHEN I was going to get to it."

"You don't have to be mean."

"And you don't have to nag me about it. Good grief. I can see it, too!"

"Fine. Do whatever you want. I don't care."

By this point, I'm out of sorts and start defending myself—which is ridiculous because I never said I wouldn't do it! In fact, I've told her before I WOULD do it. Then she gets hurt and walks away.

I let her cool off some and then I have to go apologize for getting angry and she's still not satisfied. I'm just a jerk, and I don't do anything around here.

Today though, the post gets done. I turn off the breaker, and we get to digging. Or I dig and my son moves dirt around in the hole.

"You know the objective is to get the dirt *out* of the hole," I say.

"I am. I'm digging!" he grumbles at me.

"I know, but you are just knocking loose dirt down in the hole. Take a bigger bite, and it will come out in chunks."

He puts in the effort, and a satisfying shovel full of clay dirt comes out. "There you go. That's more like it."

When it's my turn to dig he comments, "Dad, you're getting bald on top."

"When you get old, hair falls off your head and starts growing on your ears."

When we step back to admire our work, I notice the lean is not caused by settled soil like I thought. The post is actually bent right near the base. Rust has started to eat into the metal.

"Crap," I mutter, "See Nebs."

"What?" Defensively, he snaps his head back frowning and shrugs his shoulders.

"CNEBS—Can't Nothing Ever Be Simple. What do you see? Why is the post leaning?"

"It's bent."

"Yeah. I thought it was just loose soil. We got more work to do." He doesn't give me any lip since by this point he's into it. I probably should replace the post, but who's got time for that? We talk about how to fix it.

"Why don't we just bend it back?" he suggests.

"It'll probably bend the post somewhere else."

"We could dig it up, tilt it and just let the underground base be angled."

"That's a good idea but a lot of digging, and I'd rather not mess with the wiring at the bottom."

He's not going to offer another idea, but I don't think he's offended. I ask, "What do you think if we use my all-saw to cut out the crease, straighten it and then fasten a piece of angle iron to hold it?"

"Ok."

I have him chip away some of the old concrete to make room for the braces we are going to add while I go get more tools. It's dark-thirty by the time we get done. I hold the flashlight while he spray paints everything black. It takes another twenty minutes to get all the tools put up. At supper, I brag on him. My wife is very happy with me.

Later on, she slips into bed and puts her cold feet on my legs. I'm not bothered. Sex crosses my mind, but she's out of it. *Maybe in the morning*, I think, remembering it will be Saturday. I coach soccer at ten. Need to mow. Then I'll need to finish filling in the dirt, sow some grass seed, and figure out how to camouflage the angle iron and pipe clamps on the post.

--END--

Guest

"Lupe found a stiffie. 237."
"Crap. Call Campbell."
"She's a wreck."
"Seriously?"
"Not the stiff—Lupe!"
"Oh. Ok, then you talk to Lupe, and I'll call Campbell. 237?"
"Yeah."

Like the steel desk he sat behind, Clive Owens was old, heavy and showing wear on the edges. He picked up the hefty ebony desk phone and called the funeral home, "Mr. Campbell please...No, I'll wait." Clive owned the motel and his office was a converted guest room cluttered with the drift of years.

The white-faced clock with straight black hands and one sharp red rectangle above the twelve showed five minutes after ten. It was Thursday, and the summer season was drawing to a close. He reached to start a game of solitaire on the computer and knocked over a small framed photo of him and his wife. He set it right.

"Mr. Campbell. This is Owens at Ocean View. I've got a dead guest...That would be great."

Next, he called the police. "Hello, this is Clive Owens at the Ocean View motel on Shoreline. I have a dead guest and need you to send someone out...No lights please."

Owens wore nice clothes, but they were far enough out of style to be making a comeback. He wiped his palm across his bald head and went looking for the housekeeper Lupe and his manager Cindy. He found them in Cindy's office in the laundry room. Lupe in her light blue and white uniform sat on the tiny office's only guest chair. Her face was buried in her hands. Cindy knelt before her trying to soothe her.

Owens liked Cindy. She dressed and conducted herself as a professional, and she managed the motel well. Her position cut into the profit margin but allowed Clive to avoid the people and just do the tasks he liked to do. Mostly, he made purchases, did payroll and kept a game of solitaire going.

"You about done here?" Owens asked Cindy.

She looked up with a frown and shook her head. "She's upset. Totally surprised her."

"Yeah, I get that, but I've got some other things to get to."

Lupe whimpered something in Spanish. Cindy patted her on the shoulder and said gently, "You can stay in here."

"If you can't finish your round then tell Maxine," Owens said to the huddled housekeeper. Cindy's eyes, then her mouth, opened wide in disbelief.

As they headed toward room 237, Owens asked Cindy, "What? I thought I was being nice to remind her that Maxine could cover for her."

"I've already told Maxine."

"Good. Is it a mess?"

"I just had time to look in. The guest was Darlene Winsett from Duluth, Georgia. Forty-something years old. Traveling alone. Two nights."

"Business or pleasure?"

"Sales, I suppose."

As they passed through the lobby, two uniformed officers came in. Owens walked toward the taller white one. "I'm the owner. Can you have your partner park around back? We were just going to the room." Owens was anxious to get the police out of sight as quickly as possible. He didn't want guests to see anything disconcerting as they passed through the lobby.

"Sure," the officer said, and nodded to his partner, then asked Owens, "What room?"

Owens glanced around the room for eavesdroppers and said in a hushed voice, "Two-thirty-seven."

"Two-thirty-seven," the cop said to his exiting partner loud enough for others to hear. Owens grimaced.

Owens waddled down the hallway after the three exited the elevator on the second floor. He moved energetically and paused for a furtive look up and down corridor before swiping his key card. The room was cold, and the AC rattled to take the credit. A pile of clean towels lay on the floor where Lupe had dropped them. *Damn*, thought Owens, *Gonna have to wash those now.*

Darlene Winsett lay on her right side with her face toward the door. The combination of half-open eyes and complete motionlessness confirmed her demise. The officer took the lead and stepped toward the body. He knelt down to exam her face. Owens leaned over his shoulder to look for stains or blood. A rap at the door made Cindy flinch. It was the other officer.

"Could be natural," the first cop said.

The latecomer looked and said, "Yeah, but you never know, do you?"

"Nope."

"Can you boys clear her out of here pretty soon?" Owens asked.

"As quick as we can, sir," the second officer said.

"It's just that I've got guests," Owens murmured.

The policemen didn't respond. Owens looked at Cindy but found no sympathy there either.

Owens left the room saying to himself, "Campbell, I can count on. He'll bring the van instead of the hearse." He remembered what an ordeal it was in the past to deal with the death of a guest. "Not discreet at all," he mumbled after punching the elevator button. "Why the hell ambulances have to have lights and sirens to come get a corpse is beyond me." But a change in local ordinance allowed the police and a medical examiner to decide on a preliminary cause of death, and so long as there was no reason to suspect foul play or suicide, the funeral home could take the body right away. As the elevator descended, Owens consoled himself, "Campbell is about the business. He knows the deal. That's why I can count on him."

Jeffery, a lanky high school dropout, was working the front desk. Owens slipped passed him into the tiny office behind the counter to wait for Campbell. The small room gave the desk clerk a place to sit down and doubled as the security room. Owens decided to review the tapes from the night before. He enjoyed watching the recordings on high speed so that everyone darted in, wiggled around and flew off. He imagined how much money he would be making if people did come and go to Ocean View that rapidly.

He pulled up the lobby tape from the day before and started looking for the guest in 237. Jeffery leaned into the room, pointed to the phone on the desk, "Miss Cindy for you."

"Yeah," Owens said into the handset.

"The medical examiner is here. Do you want to come up?"

"No. I'm good. Try to get them to hurry."

"I don't want to be in here."

"Have any of the guests noticed anything?"

"I don't think so. We're all inside."

"Ok, good. Let's keep it that way."

"You want me to stay in here while they examine her?" she asked incredulously.

"Oh. No. No. I was just saying it's good no one noticed."

Cindy didn't respond so Owens continued, "What time did she check in yesterday?"

"I don't know. Jeffery worked. He might remember, or he can look it up." Her voice was devoid of emotion.

Owens continued, "Oh, one more thing. The police will want to contact her next of kin. Let's try to have her in Campbell's van before then, ok?"

"Sure."

"Don't want to have to wait while they figure out which funeral home to use."

Again Cindy didn't respond. Owens hung up. He grunted at Jeffery through the open door, "What time was check-in yesterday for 237?"

"What, sir?"

"What, are you daft, boy? What time did the broad in 237 check in yesterday?"

Jeffery clacked on the keyboard. "Seven fifteen p.m., sir. Paid with a business credit card."

Owens turned back to the video screens. He had the recording start playing the lobby tape at 7:00 p.m. and used the fast forward button. On the black and white monitor people teleported through the lobby, and he grinned. At 7:12 p.m. a middle aged woman in a business suit darted in, and Owen put playback to normal speed. She looked like a sales rep. She had two bags. One was obviously for business, and the other for personal items and clothing. She didn't smile or speak except when spoken to. She leaned on the counter and then did something with her feet like she was squashing a bug, but the counter blocked Owens's view.

With the thought of guests complaining about bugs, Owens felt himself start to sweat, but then he remembered the circumstances. "She won't be making any complaints," he said to ease his mind.

After signing in, she ducked below the counter, and upon rising, put her shoes on top of her rolling personal bag. She walked barefoot toward the elevator. He switched to the hall view on the second floor and saw her charcoal figure move down the corridor and into 237.

From the lobby, Owens heard Campbell's familiar voice as he greeted Jeffery.

Owens stepped out, interrupting the pleasantries between the two, "I really appreciate you getting down here so quick. Err—you brought the van?"

Campbell nodded.

"Parked at the end, right?"

Campbell again nodded.

"Good, good. I would like you to get on up there to 237 and do what you can to get the body. The medical examiner is already here and will hopefully let us get that room cleaned up. I'll call Cindy and let her know you're coming up and make sure she joins you."

Compliant Campbell nodded.

Owens went back into the office and called 237. He indulged his penchant for accelerated people and pressed fast forward on the hallway video.

"Officer Rogers," came the answer.

"Yeah. This is Clive Owens. May I speak to Cindy?"

"She's not here. Left a little while after the M.E. got here."

"Ok, thanks."

Owens dialed her office as gray ghosts floated up and down the motel hallway. On the fifth ring a weary sounding Cindy answered, "Yes?"

"Why are you in your office? Is Lupe still there, or did she get back to work?"

"Mr. Owens, what do you want?"

"Ok, never mind. I need you to go back to the room and take care of Mr. Campbell. Do what you can to get them–"

Cindy interpreted, "To hurry up, right? That's what's important. Get 'em in and get 'em out."

"Exactly. I'll be there in a minute myself."

"Great," she said flatly and hung up.

"Jeffery! Print me off the registration info for room 237."

"Yes sir, Mr. Owens." A moment later the printer was spitting out paper. "Will she be staying for her second night?"

"What?"

"I was just wondering if she will be staying for tonight. She's booked for…"

Owens cut him off, "Boy, she's dead. Check her out."

Jeffery needed a moment to process the information. He took a breath to ask a question but then just went back to the computer. "Sir. I checked her out, but housekeeping hasn't checked off on the room yet."

"Yes, I know. Have one of the girls be on standby. I'll call you."

Owen turned back to the surveillance feed to turn it off and noticed Darlene Winsett dart out of her room and toward the elevator. The timestamp showed 12:44 a.m. He put the playback speed to normal and switched to the second-floor elevator camera. She stood at the vending machine in rumpled pajamas. Her hair was down and unkempt.

Owens thought, *Midnight snacking ain't helping your figure, lady,* as he saw a bag of peanuts fall down the machine. He watched her return to the room then he turned off the feed and headed upstairs.

Cindy and Campbell stood outside the door. Owens whispered, "Are they about done?"

Cindy's lips tightened into a thin line. Campbell said, "The medical examiner is leaning toward natural causes."

Owens said, "Good, then we can get going," before two taps on the door and a swipe of his key. Darlene Winsett had been turned on her back and a bed sheet was draped over her. Officer Rogers was standing near the door, and the other officer was seated across the room.

The M.E. didn't look like a doctor at all to Owens. Thirty-something in sandals and board shorts. He was flipping through papers on a clipboard. Officer Rogers introduced them.

The doctor asked, "Mr. Owens, did you know the deceased?"

"No, but I've seen her lying around here before."

No one laughed.

"Do you know if she had any guests or visitors or showed any indications of distress or substance use?"

"None of the staff saw anything," Owens said as if he had asked, then added, "I watched her check in on the surveillance video. She looked fine. You know these sales reps have a lot of stress. Probably a heart attack, don't you think?"

"That's just the thing, we found an appointment card for her primary care doctor in Duluth that was dated for last week. I called her doctor." Looking at the clipboard, the unshaven Medical Examiner recited his notes, "Saw her PCP for a depressed mood last week. Normal BP. No temp. Slightly overweight. No history of heart disease, diabetes or high BP. No medication allergies but allergic to peanuts..."

His voice trailed on for a moment. "Her throat is swollen and there are signs of asphyxiation, but I can't say why—"

Owens interrupted, "Well, I guess when it's your time to go, it's your time to go. Do you think you can let Mr. Campbell get her body to more suitable accommodations?"

"I suppose so. Once we get in touch with the family, I'm going to suggest an autopsy."

Owens suppressed his enthusiasm and said, "Thank you, doctor."

Mr. Campbell went down for the gurney, while Cindy and Owens gathered Darlene Winsett's belongings. Owens found an empty bag of peanuts on the floor of the closet. Unobserved, he tucked it into the suitcase with her clothes.

Owens went back to the lobby with Darlene Winsett's possessions and told Jeffery, "Run up to 237 and help Cindy. I'll run the desk. Tell Cindy to have housekeeping clean the room when everybody clears out."

Owens locked the bags in a closet where they would stay until family arrived to collect them or notified the motel where to ship them. It was 4:23 p.m. and guests were starting to arrive for the weekend. Just a few minutes later, a young couple walked in the front doors giggling at each other. The man said, "We don't have reservations but just kind of came down here on the spur of the moment. We saw the sign said, No Vacancy but just thought we'd check if you might have a room open. Do you?" It was always mixed emotions for Owens when the motel was full and someone wanted a room—then it hit him.

"Well, actually we had a guest check out early. If you just need one night or don't mind to stay in a different room tomorrow night, we can accommodate you and the missus."

The woman playfully punched the man in the shoulder. "Just one night is all we'll need," he said and the lovebirds snickered.

"It will take a little while for housekeeping to get it ready, but if you don't mind, I'll go ahead and book you into room 237."

Jeffery returned to his post about thirty minutes later looking ashen and perspiring. Owens asked, "Did the room get cleared?"

The young man nodded.

"Housekeeping done?"

Another nod.

"Great. Those sweethearts sitting in the lobby are registered. Get them some keys."

Owens raided the staff refrigerator and retreated to his office on the far side of the motel. On his way, he passed Lupe in the hallway. Her face was puffy and red.

She averted her eyes but said, "*Pendejo.*"

"Good night," Owens replied.

As he had done every night for years, he locked the door behind him, stripped to his underwear, and played solitaire. Gradually the sounds of the motel grew quieter and quieter. The room was dark except for the glow of the monitor and the hallway light creeping under the door.

At 10:30 p.m., he picked up the photo of him and his wife with one hand and took the phone with the other. In the picture they stood in front of their home of forty-eight years. He punched a number in, and the phone screeched a three-note tone. Then a woman said, "The number you have dialed is disconnected or is no longer in service. Please check your listing and try again." Before she could repeat herself, Owens said, "Hey, honey. I'm working late, so I'm going to stay here tonight. I love you."

He hung up the phone before it could squawk again and stared at the photo. He had hair then and his white T-shirt and yard-work slacks hung loosely on his thin frame. Mrs. Owens was a dark-haired and dark-eyed beauty. She wore a worn sun dress and a brilliant smile. In her hand were some small paint brushes and she leaned on the mailbox newly decorated with colorful flowers. The address on the mailbox, neatly painted in her loving script, was 237 Swanson.

--END--

Crazy

My doctor says I'm crazy. Well, he's not really my doctor; he's my psychiatrist. And I guess he doesn't say I'm crazy; he says I have hallucinations which means I'm psychotic, and that is just a technical term for crazy. I don't feel crazy—most of the time.

I do admit there are times I don't think I feel normal. I get pretty down. It's not sad, so much as empty. Sad is bad, but it is better than empty. My life looks pretty empty, too. I'm forty-seven years old, and I never got married. Never found the right woman for me. I wasn't really looking, so I guess the truth is the right woman never found me.

I leave Dr. Kumar's office at 2:17 in the afternoon. The weather is nice. The parking lot looks like every other parking lot. I kind of like that you can't tell from where people park if they are going to the podiatrist, the cell phone place, or the shrink.

I've answered my four questions. "How are you doing? Are you having any problems? How is the medicine working? Have you had any hallucinations or suicidal thoughts?" I wish I could answer differently, but I say the same thing every time.

The first question is a trick question because I always answer it without thinking. You might imagine that my sluggish mind would have time to think, but it just says, "Fine" or "Good." Today I said "good" because I didn't dread leaving the apartment. So it was "good," as in better than the three days last week when

I turned myself back to sleep after every moment of consciousness.

Depression makes me sleep my life away. I'm not using it anyway, so I don't see it as a loss. I open the door of my Taurus. It's paid for but showing its age. The tan plastic interior is warm from the sun. Funny that you can have a car for twenty years, and it will still smell like chemicals if it gets hot enough.

I pull out of the manicured office complex and onto a side street. I prefer the less congested streets. When Dr. Kumar asks me if I'm having any problems, I want to say, "Yes! I don't have a job, I've got no friends, and I hate coming here!" but I don't. I wouldn't hire me or be my friend either. That's why Medicaid pays Dr. Kumar sixty three dollars for our ten minute medication management appointments. I'm so pathetic I have to get the government to pay for someone to talk to me. That's funny.

Instead, I follow the script and twaddle on about how I'm sleeping and eating and taking my medications. Dr. Kumar is especially interested in any medication side effects. Question number three is his favorite question. I fancy that I can tell when he's been to some kind of training or read a research article because he will tune in to very particular things—like bad dreams or buzzing fingernails. Dr. Kumar is smart.

I'm smart, too. Before the depression immobilized me, I had a job. I'm educated as an engineer. But why build, fix or improve anything if it's all pointless anyway? My problem is not lack of intelligence. It's motivation. I think. And maybe difficulty making decisions. Crap. That's on the symptom list for depression. Sometimes I imagine that if I could rewrite the symptoms in the diagnostic manual, then my life would change.

Doctors listen to you, but they also look at you. Dr. Kumar is perhaps less circumspect in his visual evaluation than a native American. I don't mean Native American like a Choctaw. I mean native to American culture. When he's looking at you, you can tell.

The traffic light in front of me turns amber, and my foot stretches for the brake before I have to think about it. No wonder I'm depressed! Thinking takes so much damn energy! Ugh.

Question number four was interesting today. I started to tell him some fictional but elaborate plan about how I was going to off myself with bug spray and kite string, but those kind of jokes will get you sent right off. No joking with Dr. Kumar.

"Have you had any thoughts about hurting yourself or seen or heard anything that probably wasn't real?" Dr. Kumar asked.

The question made its way through the sludge of my mind. I started talking before I knew what I would wind up saying, "No, I guess I will stick around until you can cure me."

"And any hallucinations?"

No fair! I thought, *you turned question number three in to number three part A and part B*. Out loud I said, "Well, are you still counting odors as psychosis?"

"If there is no physical reason for those odors to be there, I am."

"Well, since our last visit, I have smelled God twice."

"I see." he nodded unperturbed, "And does it still smell like trees?"

"Well, actually it smells like a forest when a breeze of crisp air blows through. It alternates between organic musty to ...to..." I struggled for the words.

Dr. Kumar is not an unkind man; besides we still had seven more minutes to our session, so he lets me fumble for the terms.

"It's back and forth between a woodland mustiness and arctic clean. Well, maybe not arctic but high mountain freshness. And it may not be a smell so much as the astringency of clean air."

"I see. Did it bother you?"

"Bother me? No, it never bothers me. It reminds me of a different world than the one I live in." One scrip and one appointment card later, I'm heading home.

I park my car in the spot reserved for 14A. That's me. The nut job in 14A. Four rooms of plain. Would a woman see it as a blank canvas needing her feminine touch? Or would she diagnose an empty soul?

Between the curb and my apartment door, the depression pounces on me. My heart gets heavy like it's sinking in my chest. The dark domain awaits. It is both refuge and prison. Within those walls I am alone but safe from a world rushing past me. I remember the time I drove my thirteen-year-old nephew through Atlanta on I-75 at forty miles an hour. I about got us killed, but I could not will myself to speed up. Jason was cool about it. He just sat there looking at the big city buildings and didn't seem to care about the flashes of painted metal blowing by us.

The depression draws up failure after failure, both old and new, illustrating my powerlessness to change anything. It sneers at the medicine and distills my life into two options: continue in hell or die. By the time I get the door unlocked, my limbs feel like they are swollen with paralyzing toxins.

The door creaks open with me leaning my weight on the knob, and I step into the gloomy room. The shades are drawn. The lights are off. I hear the refrigerator running. I close the door and slump on the couch and sit in the darkness where I have sat for days before. Nothing moves.

Then I smell it. I don't feel it. Like when a wind carries something to you. I just smell forest and mountain. Must and nothing. And it's like God has just been in the room. Did we pass in the breezeway? Is He in the back room? For a moment I think to call out, "God? Is that You?" but then I remember that I'm crazy, and I don't need to incriminate myself.

I linger for a moment and try to remember life. The couch begins to pull me into its upholstered embrace. Inviting surrender. The depression weighs in with its arrogant assumption that I will just sit.

I use my molecule of strength for a feeble effort at life and get up and go over to the window above the kitchen sink. I draw up the blinds and struggle to raise the sash. I smell asphalt and Bermuda grass. "Not very God-like," I say, and I think about opening the sliding doors to the balcony also. Sometime soon I will.

--END--

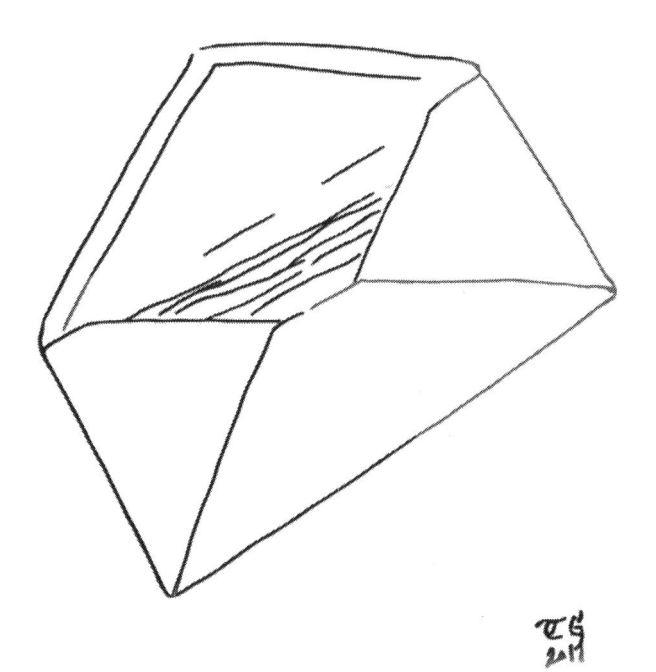

Envelope

A massive street woman stood between Otis and his glossy-black German sedan. His heart moved up to his throat to keep him from breathing. With the fear came a clenched jaw and beads of sweat. She was tall even with a slight stoop and bulky torso, wearing a tattered olive-green parka. It was August and Otis could smell the sourness of old sweat.

Moments before, his day had been going much better. He had left the office a little early with a lie that he wanted to try to avoid rush hour traffic. Really, he was hoping to score some cash. Some nut job had been hiding yellow envelopes full of cash around downtown Nashville. Otis was a very intelligent man, and while he couldn't account for all the envelopes, he noticed enough of a pattern to expect one of the cash caches to be on the west side of a street running north-south.

Before he had encountered the street woman, he had been cruising slowly down the delivery alley, avoiding battered trash cans and looking to his left. "Hey Jude" was playing on the radio, but Otis wasn't paying attention to anything that wasn't yellow. The song faded out before ending and the smoothest male voice said, "Hey, you're listening to WKPW. Nashville's local news leader! This town is still buzzing with excitement over plain yellow envelopes."

The announcer's female counterpart Erin said, "That's right, Chris. Those simple yellow envelopes contain hundreds of dollars in cash! We've been reporting on finds from five hundred to five thousand dollars! But who knows how many finders never say a thing?"

"Hey, I'd just take the cash and run." Chris said. "Nothing wrong with finding five thousand dollars. And if your bummy friends don't know, they can't ask you to borrow it!"

"Yeah, considering your friends, I'd keep it to myself too," laughed Erin.

"Erin, have you been out looking? Now tell the truth."

Still giggling she said, "Actually, I've had my eye out."

"Yeah, you, me, and everybody else." Then to his listeners, Chris said, "If you've got a theory on the Mysterious Mister Moneybags we'd love to hear it. Post your ideas on our Facebook page or send us an email."

"I can't say what it's done for downtown businesses, but envelopes of cash have certainly increased downtown traffic," Erin segued to the traffic report. Otis's car rolled slowly down the access lane as bits of gravel crunched under the tires.

That's when Otis saw it—a tiny yellow sliver on the front of a dark green dumpster. Suppressing his excitement, he sprang out of his car leaving the door open. Because the envelope was about an inch thick, he had to really tug to get it free. That just made him all the more eager, but he was careful not to tear the yellow paper. He finally pulled it free.

He was so focused on his find that he didn't notice the homeless woman approach from behind. He was startled by her presence when he turned around to head to his car. She was close enough to jump into his vehicle and close the door before he could stop her. If she wanted, she could stop him from doing the same.

Distance-wise they were four yards apart, but in every other way they were miles apart. Otis had smooth skin and well-groomed hair. The woman was dark with sun and dirt. Gray hair spilled out from under a large hat like a science fair project gone wrong. Otis wore four-hundred-dollar navy-blue suit pants and a white pinstriped shirt to match—still crisp with starch. She was wrapped in layer after layer of cast-off clothing. It made Otis feel some better when he noticed that she was not as heavy as her bulky clothing made her first appear.

"Hi," she smiled. "My name is Nediva. Pleased to meet you."

Otis didn't know what to say. "Hello, I'm Otis Watkins with Jamison, McDougal and Howell," didn't seem right at all.

"Hi," he said.

Nediva grinned at him. Her eyebrows raised like she expected him to ask her a question. His car idled quietly in the background. He looked at the car and back at her. In his right hand, he clutched the yellow envelope. A dozen options and ideas raced through his mind. *She wants the envelope; there are hundreds of dollars in there! It's worth a fight. Maybe she doesn't know about the money. Do homeless people even listen to the news? Does she look like she's on drugs? What does she want? I can shove her out of the way and get to the car. Maybe I can give her some of the money. Is there anyone else here?*

That last thought brought him back to the street. They were remarkably alone. Traffic moved by in fits and starts on the other side of the buildings around them. There were no deliveries this time of day.

"Hey, hey, how about I give you something," Otis stammered. His initial thought was to open the envelope and give her part of it, but as he brought it forward it occurred to him that if she saw the contents of the packet she might not be content with just a little bit. So without stopping the movement of his right arm, he stuffed the envelope into his front pocket and reached around with his left hand for his wallet.

Nediva just watched him and wondered if the left hand knew what the right hand was doing.

Thank God I keep that one hundred dollars in my wallet! he thought.

Otis pulled out the slick ostrich leather bi-fold and opened it up. Inside was a crisp one-hundred-dollar-bill. He opened it up wide so she could see there was no more cash inside.

With his arm straight like the cash was a fencer's foil, Otis stepped toward her and said, "Here, take this."

Nediva cocked her head and reached out her hand. Before the bill had settled into her palm, Otis was in the car and driving off. On the way home, he would discover the envelope in his pocket was full of buy-one-get-one-free coupons for fast food. They were the best sort; the kind with no expiration dates.

After he pulled away, Nediva dug down deep through layers and layers of protective clothing and pulled out a one-gallon baggie full of crisp yellow envelopes. Some had antiseptic wipes, others had gift certificates, or directions to soup kitchens or shelters. A couple had keys to bus station lockers stuffed with clean socks and underwear. She opened one already full of cash and stuck Otis's hundred-dollar-bill in among the others. Then Nediva started looking for a place she could hide it.

--END--

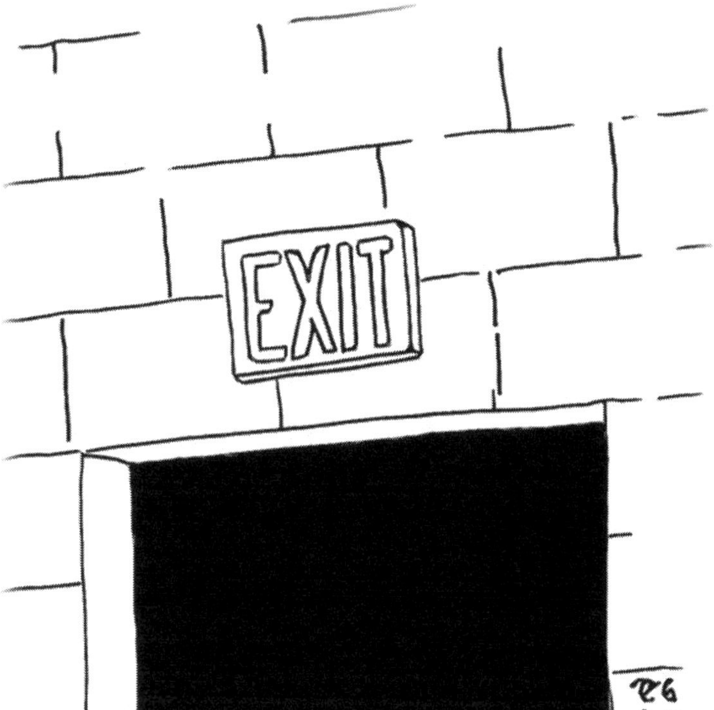

EXIT
2017

Exit

Nobody ever thinks about an exit strategy. I don't have one and I'm pretty sure I'm going to die for it. I'm trapped in the sunken rear doorway of Crystal's Creations on the back side of Twin Pines shopping center. It's dark except for one humming, orange light pole. I have a gun, but the cops have guns, too. Just minutes ago, everything hit the fan.

I met Shine a few months back around the time I quit school. I don't think Shine is her real name, but it's the only one she goes by. She calls me her boy toy, but she ain't that much older than me. We met at a party I wasn't even supposed to be at. My buddy Brent had heard about it. We thought it was a college party, but I don't think any of the folks there went to college. Some of them was way too old and the other ones didn't strike me as the college type. Shine didn't look like a college chick either, but that's ok. I ain't into all that.

She had the side of her head shaved and some of the rest dyed blue. That's the way I remember her, but she could comb the long parts over the shaved side and not look like such a party girl. And her tattoos were not that noticeable with regular clothes on. That night, though, she had on black lace and leather. I came in the front door and noticed her straight away leaning up against the far wall talkin' to a girlfriend. She was hot in a metallic mini skirt and biker boots. I thought we made eye contact, but I figured it was just my imagination.

I don't even know whose house it was, but a party is a party. When Brent and I walked in, a couple of people in the living room looked at us, then went back to whatever they was doing. Something in the air made my eyes burn as I followed Brent through the crowd toward the kitchen. That's where the keg was set up. I turned to take another look at Shine. She was already right up next to me.

"You ain't supposed to be here," she said plainly and loud enough to be heard over the music. My eyes turned toward Brent, but he had gone on to the kitchen. "We was invited. My friend Brent said we was invited." I hoped the music covered the shake in my voice.

"Yeah? Who you know here?"

I didn't know a soul 'cept Brent, and we wasn't that close. She looked at me with a bitty smile, then leaned in close enough for me to feel the heat of her face and smell cigarettes then whispered, "Wanna have some fun?"

I dropped some kind of pills she had, and we hooked up at some point. That night is a bit of a blur. After that, though, we was a couple even if she wouldn't say so. She sort of took me in. She was so exciting to be with. I've never been around someone with such a thing for thrills. We was always going and doing something. She had connections with all kinds of peeps, from teen keggers, to blown-out pot heads, to serious biker dudes. And those dudes scared me. Crank was one of them. He's the reason I'm where I am now.

Twin Pines never has a lot of people and this time of night is usually all but dead. Crystal's Creations is in the middle of a row of eight stores. There is a title loan place on one end and a pizza place too. That's where me and Crank was earlier. I'm pretty sure there is a cop to my right somewhere. In front of me is a chain link fence covered over with vines and a patch of woods on the other side. If I can get there, I can make it.

I don't know how Shine and Crank met, but I got the feeling they was involved somehow in the past. Me and Shine had been doing some running for him. Mostly small deliveries. Nobody ever said what we was delivering. Between the pay and the contacts, we was living party to party.

#

"We need to come up with some cash," Shine said. Her half blonde, half blue hair was smoothed down and shaped to points like icicle daggers. We'd been staying at her half-brother's apartment after we burned bridges with my parents, her uncle and a guy we hardly knew. In that order, I might say. And now her brother had been complaining that if we was not going to pay rent then he ought not to have to come home to a wrecked house.

"What do we need cash for?" I asked. She took a draw from a cigarette. She didn't look as tired as usual. The night before we had actually fixed a meal and didn't drink that much. It was a nice bit of regular. That's how she's kept me going: just enough crazy to be exciting and just enough normal to keep me from freaking out. And she was gorgeous. Even with muddy makeup and bits of puke on her clothes, she still gets to me. Today, except for the cigarette, she could be a regular TV mom. Her face was clean, and her eyes was a bright open sky.

"Mosey Joe's party. There's gonna be a cover charge for the beer and weed, and if I was screwing him he'd let me in free but not you."

I flinched at the "screwing him." I can't never tell if she says shit like that to threaten me or if she just don't care. I do care. Maybe it's because she's my first serious girlfriend. Or maybe it's because she is the hottest chick I've ever been with. Whatever, I don't know, but to me she is my girlfriend, and I care, even if she calls me an idiot for using the word.

"Any ideas?" I ask.

"Too bad we don't get paid for your dopey looks."

"Aw, don't be like that."

"Well, you're a prick. I'm always having to cover for you."

"How can I keep a job and keep up with you?" I argued.

"Maybe you don't need to keep. Up. With. Me." She said the last words slowly. That bit of anger in me faded with the thought of her leaving. If it wasn't for the sex, and apparent faithfulness on her part, I'd have a hard time not thinkin' she just wanted me for transportation and as a side thang.

"I want to keep up with you," I halfway tried to make it into a sexual innuendo, but past shoot-downs kind of dampened my mojo.

"Then quit being a ass and think of where we can get fifty bucks," she said. I had no idea. No part-time jobs was gonna pay that on the first day. She read my mind it seemed and snapped, "And Burger King ain't gonna meet our schedule. What about your grandma?"

The idea made me feel like I was chewin' on cardboard. We had taken some money from my grandma Sweeny, who I call Granny Sween, a few months back. We hadn't had a chance to pay it back yet, though.

"I don't know. Last time we said we was just gonna borrow—"

"I guess I could make a booty call to Mosey. Maybe get me in."

"Damn, Shine! You got me stealing from my grandmother."

"She's a bitch and you know it. Besides she don't need it. She's got plenty."

We got breakfast and went over to Granny Sween's. I was supposed to talk to Granny so Shine could sneak in through the side window. I rapped on the back door of her rental house and walked in. As usual, she was sitting in her recliner.

"Hey granma, I got you some breakfast." I held up the white paper bag, "A bacon biscuit with the bacon on the side."

"That girl with you?"

I didn't know if Shine could hear me. but surely she hadn't had time to get inside. "No granma. Just me."

"Didjoo bring my money back or just this damn biscuit?"

"I just wanted to bring you breakfast." She had no idea the biscuit was gonna cost her a hundred bucks or however much was in her top dresser drawer.

Granny Sween got some checks that covered her living expenses and pretty much kept to herself. Until my buddies in fifth grade started talking about Thanksgiving plans, it never occurred to me that most people spend holidays with grandparents. She never did nothing to have people over. She was sour on everything. I don't think she really even wanted to live, but she kept on anyway.

I handed the biscuit to her. The paper was kind of loose 'cause I had forgotten she didn't like her bacon in the biscuit until Shine had reminded me. So on the way over I separated them and rewrapped it, hoping Granny wouldn't notice. She did.

"Somebody's been into this."

"I forgot to tell 'em to keep it separate until—" I cut myself off. Mentioning Shine was a big no no. "So, I pulled it apart the way you like it."

Fingertips up, like a preacher holding Jesus' bread, she held the bacon in one hand and the biscuit in the other and started to eat. The TV was on but the sound was off, and I wanted to give some cover for Shine. "Where's your remote?" I asked.

With her bacon hand she picked it up and handed it to me. The grease made the volume button a little slippery. A talk show was on and I turned it up in time for someone to say, "... right after this break." A makeup commercial was up next. Granny munched on without talking as crumbs fell away from her near toothless mouth.

"Get me some coffee." She nodded at her mug on the end table.

The kitchen was dark and the black coffee pot fit right in with the shadows. I could hear Shine rustling the blinds in the back bedroom. When I carried the mug back to Granny Sween and set it on the end table, a loud thump came from the back of the house.

"What was that? What was that?" Granny said and started to rise. Without thinking, I put my hand on her shoulder. It was just enough resistance to sit her back down. Dropping the remains of the biscuit and bacon, Granny Sween clutched on the recliner arms to pull herself upright. I panicked at the thought of her confronting Shine in the bedroom and I pushed her down again, "Granny, it was just the TV."

She glared up at me, "The TV my ass! Somebody's back there!" I could hear more soft thuds and rattles from the bedroom. Granny tried to stand up again. This time when I pushed her back in the chair she landed hard enough to jar the table and spill some of the coffee. "Ok granma. I'll go look." I headed toward the back door.

"Why you little twerp. I'm gonna switch your thievin' ass!"

"Sorry granny!" I said and left through the door I had come in. I felt bad, but me and Shine laughed about it later in the car. That money didn't last long and we didn't try again cause she was on to us. So the next time we needed cash, we asked Crank for some extra work.

"Thing is you guys ain't serious about it," he said. He wore a motorcycle vest with patches on it—skulls and ravens—to match his tattoos.

"I'm serious..." I said.

Shine cut me off, "Shut the hell up, boy. You don't know what you're talking about." She lowered her eyes to look directly at Crank, "This is for real."

Crank returned the stare, "That's right. No more of this penny-ass stuff. If you want in then you got to be in and on the clock so to speak."

"What you mean, "on the clock?" My nervousness was showing through. Up till now I could act like I didn't know what was in the bags. I was just driving Shine over to some random house and she'd hop out and come right back. Still, I knew Crank was ambitious to make more of his own money and that meant increasing his trade and his trade was drugs whether anybody ever said it or not.

"I mean, not just when you need cash but I'll pay you by the week or by the job but either way you can't just come and go. You are either with me regular, or you ain't with me at all."

Shine said, "So you gonna pay us a salary?"

"Maybe, but I don't care to pay you by the job just so long as you know you are on the hook for at least four drops a week." Shine continued to negotiate, but I couldn't get the image of me on Crank's hook out of my mind.

From then on, we was spending several hours a week transporting stuff for Crank. The scary ones were the out-of-state hauls. I thought we was going to die the second time. I'd never seen so many guns in my life. Shine was always cool though. The big dudes were all business, but the small timers would make suggestive comments and she would flirt back. I couldn't help but feel jealous. After trading a bag of cash for two huge duffels of weed in Texas, we was driving back to Tennessee.

"Why you gotta be like that?" I asked her. "You don't have to come on to them dirt bags."

"Why do you have to be such a dumb ass? It's all business."

"I don't like it."

"Then get over it. We got tons of green doing shit jobs and you want to whine about the way some guy looks at my ass? Grow up!" She lit a cigarette to say, "Conversation over."

I should have dropped it; instead I said, "It's not them, it's you—I can handle them being all creep but you don't have to bend over and say shit like how heavy these bags are."

"Let me tell you something. Those guys don't give a fried flip about you or me. If me being nice-nice makes things go smoother then so what? Do you realize that every time you go snarling at me they notice that we are more than just freakin' co-workers? That puts us in danger, you dumb ass. These guys don't play, and if I'd know'd you were going to be such a cry baby about it, then I'd left you at a daycare."

My feelings, as always, was up in a mess. She, if somewhat indirectly, acknowledged that we were actually more than co-workers which made me feel good, but she wasn't gonna stop the show. And she had a good point about letting others see I cared for her. "You're right, Shine. It's hard, but I'm gonna work on it." She nodded at me. Then I added, "For you." She rolled her eyes and blew smoke out the window.

#

The tops of the trees are flashing blue. The building keeps the rest in shadows below that. I crouch as low as I can and peek toward the cop. My heart knocks on the base of my skull. He's slowly walking toward me and using his flashlight to peek into each of the back doors on the shopping center. I've got maybe three minutes.

That's what Crank said.

"Three minutes—in and out, tops," Crank was explaining to Shine. I was still trying to figure on another option than robbing the Quik-Cash. Someone had stolen a lot of weed from Crank and he was eight hundred dollars short on his payment to his distributor. He had the half purple-yellow face to show for it. They gave him twenty-four hours to get them the money. So Crank figured we'd get most of that from the

Quik-Cash and a few hundred extra from hitting Ace's Pizza. "Might as well get two for one," he said.

I was not convinced, "I'm not sure this is such a good idea—"

As usual Shine snapped, "You never think anything is a good idea."

"Can't we just raise some prices—"

Now it was Crank's turn to interrupt. "You can't raise shit! If not for having to hold your hand on the drop in Louisiana I would have been here and not gotten my shit stolen." He stood up and looked right at me, "You owe me, and if they is gonna mess me up then I'm going to mess you up first."

Shine's eyebrows came down and together. I hoped it was for me. She said, "Hey, Crank. He's in. He's in. He's just scared, that's all. He's gonna do it." She turned to me, "You're going to do it, ain't you?" but didn't give me time to respond. "So you was saying. You know the cash box is not in the safe until ten. There will be only one person working and the rules are to not fight but give the cash and push the panic button?"

"Yeah, I have a customer who worked there. Only thing we got to worry about is the cameras. No way to take them out so we just got to be quick in and quick out—Quik-Cash!" and he and Shine started laughing. Cold sweat and a stomach roll was my reaction. I've never robbed anyone, and Crank was saying guns was the only way to get them to take you seriously.

Being as it was late November, it was dark by 5:00 p.m. Crank had "borrowed" a tagless beater from some pill head that owed him. Shine would drive. She'd pull up. We'd jump out. Do the deal then Crank would either say "One" or "Two." One meant he thought the haul was enough, and we'd get back in the car and leave. "Two" meant we'd run down to Ace's.

I'd been in Quik-Cash before with a friend but never as a customer. Didn't figure I'd know anyone there, but I'd eat at Ace's lots of times. It wasn't a chain—just a local guy running deliveries and a few booths for dine-ins. We had masks.

Mine was a navy-blue ski mask. It smelled like beer and somebody else's sweat. I was soaking it with my own when Shine rolled up in front of the glass doors to the Quik-Cash. The clerk was head down messing with something behind the counter in the brightly lit room. Yellow light spilled out onto the concrete walkway. We was halfway across the room before the plump girl working the counter looked up. Crank already had his shotgun pointed at her and fear cut her squeak of surprise in half.

"Cash now or you're dead."

She was froze in fear. Dread came up in me with the vision of him blasting her right in front of me. Fear or sweat made me lose my grip on the revolver loaned to me and it thudded on the carpeted concrete. It turned out to be just enough of a distraction for the girl to come to her senses and open the drawer. No doubt the glass between us was bulletproof, but who would want to test it out with your life?

She slipped ten one-hundred-dollar bills through the opening saying, "We only keep a thousand dollars in the drawer. The rest..."

"Shut up. And lay down behind the counter." Crank growled. I was relieved no one would die.

I was so wrong.

We busted out of the doors, and Crank shouted, "Two!"

I went to the car anyway. I guess I just didn't understand.

"Two! Two! You dumb ass!" and he jerked on the back of my jacket pulling me out of the car.

He then leaned down, tossed the bills into Shine, and said, "Drive down!"

We entered Ace's full-bore, rattling the brass door chimes. And there was Adam "Ace" Abramovich himself behind the counter. An old-fashioned register sat on the glass counter. Inside the case were mints, candy and gum and cheap Italian figurines and flags for decoration.

Ace is older, maybe in his fifties, he's not a small man, but he pulled up large when Crank raised the shotgun. "All your cash now," Crank said.

Ace wiped his hands down the front of his white apron and over his big belly. "Uh. What for?" he asked. I guess people don't think straight when they are scared. I felt less afraid myself seeing fear in the girl at Quik-Cash and now Ace's.

"It's a robbery, dumb ass," I said. Ace looked at me as if he were trying to recognize me. I immediately looked away. And that's when all hell broke loose.

The door bells behind us tinkled as someone came walking in. Crank and I both turned round to see some teenage delivery boy with an insulated pizza bag and a cheesy red, white, and green ball cap. "Ace's Pizza. It's fast or it's free!" Crank blasted the boy right in the chest. The boom was deafening, and the ringing started before the guy's body settled to the floor. Crank turned back to Ace, but I saw a blinking blue flash reflect off one of the cars in the parking lot.

"Crank! We got—"

"Shut the hell up!"

"But there's—"

Boom! I turned and saw old man Ace slump down the wall behind him. Crank grabbed for the register and I looked back outside in time to see Shine drive off. She was replaced by a police patrol car. The room filled with those damned blinking blue lights.

Crank stuffed his pockets with cash and calmly said, "Hold on."

I could hear Ace sputtering behind the counter. Outside the cop was making his way toward us, gun drawn. Crank shot through the window and it busted. The room was hazy with gun smoke and my ears were screaming. The blast must have wounded the cop 'cause he was down on his butt backing up to his car. Crank racked the shotgun again and stepped toward the door. It seems odd that I don't remember hearing the cop's gun fire, but I do remember seeing the thud of the bullets hitting Crank in the chest. The next bullets were meant for me but shattered the mirrored wall. Something in me snapped and like an animal, I ran away from the danger. I found my way out the back door and into the cool air. When I heard sirens off to my left I turned right and started running along the cinder-block wall of the shopping center.

So, here I am with more and more cops pulling up out front and that one to my right closing in on me. There is a metal taste in my mouth. I must have bitten my tongue. I haven't used the revolver and it is heavy in my hand. I'm not ready, but this is my exit. I sprint for the chain link fence. I try to fire off some shots toward the approaching cop but the trigger just clicks. When I raise my right hand up to grab high on the fence, to pull myself up, the barrel of the gun snags the wire and it jerks the pistol from my hand. When something starts punching my side, I lose my grip and fall to the base of the fence. Exit fail.

#

"We have new developments in the Twin Pines shooting. Action News Five reporter Erin Louis brings this report. Erin?"

"Yes, John. It's been one month since the Twin Pines Shopping Center shooting where four people died in this normally quiet small town. According to police reports one of the suspects, Trevor Starns, was carrying an unloaded revolver. Yesterday his parents filed suit against the police department for the excessive use of force. I spoke with his mother, Jeannie Thompson, earlier today. This is what she had to say, "They didn't have to do all that to him. The gun wasn't even loaded. He was just a kid trying to get out of a bad situation."

"Meanwhile, police are still searching for a third suspect and the thousand dollars taken from the Quik-Cash. Erin Louis, Action News Five Live Report."

--END--

Blue Hydrangea

Bryce began to sweat as soon as he stepped out of his car. It was hot and muggy, typical for a Tennessee summer afternoon. He walked toward the front door of his grandmother's house, now his, feeling perplexed. She was an odd woman. "Strange old biddy" is what some of the family called her. It had been three months since her death and he was still unpacking their relationship.

Her house sat comfortably in a shaded subdivision developed in the late fifties. That's when her husband, the grandfather Bryce had never met, had died. He worked for the railroad. They had four children and twelve grandchildren. Dorothy, or "Grandma" as he called her, never remarried and raised the four kids alone while working as a secretary for a legal firm in Nashville.

The house was a pale yellow brick cottage with a steep pitched roof. The alcove over the wooden front door did its best to mimic a church steeple. The concrete walkway, sandy with age, ran straight to the front door from the street where Bryce had parked. The house faced east, and with large hardwoods providing dappled shade, it was an ideal yard for growing hydrangeas.

Bryce scanned his new possession. It looked the same, but it didn't feel the same. He and his grandmother had an emotionally-reserved relationship, but it was more of a relationship than any of his siblings or cousins had with her. She was bossy, controlling and demanding. A "harrumph" of satisfaction was the closest thing you would ever get to a "thank you" from her.

He had spent a lot of time working in the yard for her. Grass to mow. Weeds to pull. Flowers to plant. She would come out on the small uncovered porch to watch him work.

"You don't need to put that there. It's too close to the driveway," she would say.

"Ok."

"No, not there either. Look," she said holding her hands wide apart. "About this far away from the azalea."

"Ok."

"And turn it around so the good side faces the house."

"Ok."

When she would give orders from the concrete platform of the porch, Bryce always thought she looked like a little white-haired admiral on the deck of a warship barking commands. He didn't mind. He figured if you are that old, you are entitled to be a little grumpy.

Regardless of the task—whether he was mowing, raking, or planting—about fifteen minutes before he would be finished, she would quietly disappear into the house. He would just hear the clump of the heavy door close. Even though he had tried to catch her, he never once actually saw her walk inside. As he was putting the tools away and finishing up, she would return with a large glass of freshly-brewed iced tea. So sweet it would make your teeth hurt, but so smooth he would drink it in big gulps. Then they would have their little ritual.

"What do I owe you?" she would growl like she was bargaining with a horse trader, her faded eyes peering at him over her polished glasses.

"Nothing."

"Aw, come on, I owe you something," she would frown.

"It's ok, Grandma. You don't have to pay me."

"Yes I do!" she would snap back. "I might not be able to afford much, but I can pay you something. Now, I never would have worked all those years for Burke and Burke if they hadn't paid me anything." He would listen patiently while she sang the familiar song and verse.

Once when he was a teenager and in need of some cash for a weekend movie date, he went off script and said, "Twenty dollars." He thought she was going to have a stroke. "Twenty dollars?! You think I have twenty dollars? Why, I could get the neighbor kid to do that for a dollar fifty probably!"

Yeah, in nineteen fifty, Bryce thought.

Her post-work monologue would go on and on about how expensive everything was, yet how she thought it was fair to pay him for his time. The truth was since the increase in the price of gas, his trips to do her yard work were usually a net loss for Bryce.

Eventually she would put three or four dollars in his hand. Once it was twelve dollars for a full day's work. She always handed the bills over like it was a sacred ceremony. Bill by bill, she would place the money in his hands, then gently clasp her soft veiny hands around his. For just a moment he would feel the pressure of her bony fingertips pushing through soft pads of flesh. At such moments she seemed so frail.

#

Halfway up the walkway, Bryce asked himself, *Was that why I kept coming back? I just felt sorry for her?* He looked across the neatly maintained lawn. He teared up when he saw the blooming hydrangeas. She might not have loved him, but she loved those big-leafed beauties.

In fact, she wore him out over them. He knew everything there was to know about how to grow and care for hydrangeas. There were two pink ones on the left side of the house and another pink one on the right. But sticking out like an oddball was a blue one right next to it. It was smaller than the pink three because he had just planted it two years ago.

Grandma hated it. She hated blue flowers and she wanted "formal balance" in her landscape. Three pink and one blue hydrangea wasn't going to cut it for her. That blue hydrangea had been a curse for both of them. Actually, it wasn't the plant; it was the ground itself that was cursed. There had been half a dozen hydrangeas planted in the spot. After multiple failed attempts to get a pink one to grow there, Bryce had even suggested that they just plant something else.

His grandmother looked at him like he had blasphemed the Creator.

"I'm going to have two pink hydrangeas on each side of my house. And they are all going to actually be pink!"

"Yes, ma'am."

"Now let's put some stuff down and turn that rebel pink."

"Yes, ma'am."

And put some stuff down he did—every kind of additive imaginable. She even had him dig up the soil once and replace it all. They would get new varieties, even ones advertised to be guaranteed pink, only to see the color fade from pink to white to green to blue and bluer. She might have four pink hydrangeas for a couple of years, but then that one, closest to the front door, would start turning blue.

Bryce came to hate that plant. He would grumble under his breath while working on it. Sort of a reverse worship, on his knees, but offering curses rather than prayers. He fantasized about coming over at night and cutting it down. He seriously considered spray-painting it pink.

He researched online the best way to turn that infernal blue hydrangea pink, and while she didn't want to pay for it, she was always open to the latest theory or product that he suggested they try. His grandmother would watch over him from the porch as he tried the next intervention. She was always convinced of success. "We're going to get that sucker pink." And then pointing up at the sky the little admiral would add, "This time, THIS TIME, it's going to work!" Bryce was never so convinced.

As he climbed up the front steps he felt a twinge of regret that he was never able to get that one pink for her. He wiped his eye and unlocked the front door to his new home. It was neat and sparsely furnished, but comfortable. The air was stale from lack of movement and smelled like old wood. He walked into the kitchen and thought about the "reading of the will" two days prior. He went as a matter of loyalty, knowing that except for the house, she didn't really own anything, but he had wanted to hear her last wishes.

Bryce opened one of the upper cabinets nearest the stove. On the lowest shelf were a dozen light-green glasses neatly arranged two rows deep. She had served him many gallons of tea in those glasses.

At the lawyer's office, everybody was shocked to discover that "Grandma Groucy" had a savings fund of seven million dollars. With amusement, Bryce recalled the shocked faces of his aunts and uncles. He was the only grandkid present.

"I could have driven a truck into Uncle Bob's mouth," Bryce said and the empty house echoed it back. Bryce chuckled at the image and the old house seemed to join him.

An exciting buzz began to grow in the room as the lawyer got down to the details of how she wanted her property dispersed. The excitement turned sour like clothes left too long in the washer when each adult child, each grandchild and the two great-grandchildren got what amounted to one million dollars, divided equally. Her church got a million dollars and the rest, and all her property went to Bryce. "Bryce my dear grandson..." the lawyer read. The memory of those unexpected words brought unexpected tears. The tears turned angry when he thought of all the fuming and resentment and selfishness that erupted when the lawyer was done. But he cried the most when he realized he did love her and maybe she loved him back. Already, he missed her.

When his sobbing subsided, Bryce noticed it had started to rain—an afternoon thunderstorm born of high humidity and Southern heat. He hoped it would bring some relief to him and the hydrangeas which really didn't care for hot, hot. The falling rain and thunder resonated through the vacant house. He went to the front door and looked out at his car. It was difficult to see through the torrential rain. *I gotta get to the courthouse*, he said to himself and began rummaging through the hall closet looking for an umbrella.

In his search through unfamiliar things, he accidentally knocked over a small yellow bag and a spray of gray-brown pellets clicked across the hardwood floor. He picked up the plastic five-pound bag and read the label: "Horton's Soil Rite, Aluminum sulfate, Guaranteed to turn Hydrangeas blue!"

--END--

Fields

Clyde made his way toward the house just as the rain began to fall. His old barn dog Leroy had seen him off at dawn, and Clyde had been discing his farmland ever since. The dry soil had dusted him and his open-cab M Farmall tractor with a soft powdering of earth. Large, flat drops fell slowly as if reluctant to face their fate on the parched ground. The droplets splotched the old red tractor. Clyde took it all in—a field too dry to grow anything, the smell of earth and rain, and the passing thundershower that wouldn't make a difference.

As he bumped across the field, he thought of Annie, his wife of forty years. Some good times for sure, but mostly just work and doing what need be done. She had the face and figure of a good farm wife. Plain and honest and nowhere near as pretty as Jenny, the new waitress down at Mildred's Restaurant. At twenty-nine, Jenny was barely half Clyde's age but she, as they say, took a shine to him. They met on the first day of her new job.

"What can I get you fellers? Special today is hamburger steak with gravy, mashed potatoes, green beans and apples."

"Drinks included?" Clyde asked, knowing that they were. Homer Sullivan cut his eyes and grinned. Their buddy Tom added, "Yeah, I'm awful thirsty...and broke." The round-bellied, thin-haired men snickered like schoolboys.

The faint blush that crossed Jenny's face brought Clyde a sense of satisfaction.

"I'll have to go see," she said, "Be right back."

The farmers chuckled when she left. Then laughed out loud when from somewhere in the back they heard Mildred say, "Them old coots know the drinks are included." Jenny came back with a puckered grin, and Clyde felt something like new warmth from stirred coals.

Already a regular, he found himself eating at Mildred's more and more. His wife didn't mind. She didn't care to cook much anymore. Annie didn't care much about anything anymore. It was quiet and dark at home but chuckles and teasing with Jenny during lunch. And dinner was a little more intimate as his farm friends supped at home. He told himself it saved time to eat out.

One evening Jenny asked, "Hey, Mr. Stovall? It's been awful dry. Are you going to be able to get a crop in?" The concern was genuine.

"I reckon I'll be ok. It's not my first dry spring." His unassuming confidence brought a smile to her face. Clyde felt the pull again.

"So what can I get you tonight?" Jenny asked and for the first time Clyde's mind answered with a carnal thought. He took in her fair hair, pretty face and figure. She had two children of her own, but unlike Clyde's who were out of the house, Jenny was raising a teenage boy and a nine-year-old girl. In bits and pieces, she had shared with him the challenges of single-parenting and the troubles with her ex. She felt the pressure of his absence whenever a child was sick or when money was tight, but he was such a jackass over those same issues that she couldn't stomach the idea of having him back.

"Better lonely and unfulfilled than miserable," she told Clyde once. He told her she was quoting the Proverbs. She was impressed even though he couldn't remember precisely which one it was.

He knew better than to get so involved, but Jenny's authentic respect toward him and his own resentments toward Annie pulled and pushed. Already a generous person with an inclination to help his neighbors meant Clyde was soon bringing her root vegetables, kale, and cabbage from his garden and doing what he could to help her out. When her mower broke down and needed three weeks to repair, he hauled it to the co-op (and later paid the bill). When he went over to mow the overgrown yard, Clyde met her son and daughter.

"Dylan and Savannah, this is Mr. Stovall. He's going to help us with the yard," Jenny said.

"Because Dad's too big a prick to do it?" Dylan replied. Savannah lifted her head but not her eyes from the book she held with both hands.

"Nice to meet you, son," Clyde said as he nodded at the boy. "And you too, Miss." The respectful "miss" brought a flash of eye contact from the girl.

Dylan was thin and lanky. Dark jeans, a dark T-shirt and uncut hair worked as camouflage for everything but the anger.

"I've brought both my mowers." Pointing to the large wheeled push mower, Clyde asked, "Do you know how to use one of these?"

"Yeah."

"Well, I figured I'd use the zero turn, and your mom said you could handle the pushing."

Having experience limited to consumer grade equipment, Dylan looked a little intimidated by the serious machines on Clyde's trailer. Clyde pulled the oil-stained behemoth, smelling of gasoline and grass, off the trailer then steadily and plainly explained how to start and operate it. Tentatively Dylan pulled the starter cord. No fire.

"Keep at it. Harder though."

On the second pull the machine roared to life. Dylan looked satisfied. Clyde grinned at him. Then over the roar he said, "Ok! You work around the house and trees!"

Dylan had to lean into it, but he was soon manhandling the machine around the single wide trailer. Forty-five minutes and a glass of lemonade later, Clyde was heading home. His wife didn't notice he'd been gone or ask where he'd been.

#

Topping the last rise brought his equipment shed into view. It was set off some from the house but still dwarfed it in size. Built of poles and gray sheet metal it was a witness that this ground was farm land. Leroy and a few cats lived in the shed, but it was built for the machinery. One of the tractors garaged there was worth more than the house. As he jostled across the land, Clyde wondered if it was worth the effort. Farming had always been lots of work with never a guarantee of success. Bean leaf beetles three weeks prior to harvest one year had just about put them under. Clyde had to borrow a lot of money the next spring.

As the Farmall, passed on to him by his father, pulled Clyde across the fresh-plowed ground, he adjusted the green Bank of Commerce hat on his head. It was a "gift" from the bank for taking out a loan. Clyde

Fields

figured that particular hat had cost him forty-seven-thousand dollars. He wore it to get what he could from it, not because he was a fan. It was in his hand several times over the years, and it bothered him that it had to be that way to farm. He hated that his labor was not enough. His land and equipment were not enough. He had to let people who had not put a single drop of sweat into the farm eat of its monetary harvests.

The drought was making any planting a low probability enterprise. It struck Clyde as interesting that it was raining on a dry field when rains and fields had worried him most of the day. His thoughts effortlessly drifted to Jenny.

"Mr. Stovall, could you help me with my car?" Jenny asked after he finished his supper at Mildred's one evening.

"Sure, what's wrong with it?"

"It didn't start right on the way in today, and I'm afraid it won't make it home."

"Sure thing, Jenny."

It was 7:55 p.m. but still light and warm outside. Clyde worked on the car tightening cables and checking the battery acid level. Mildred closed up at 8:00 and by 8:15, Clyde and Jenny were alone in the gravel parking lot.

"Your battery is gone. The heat is hard on them. I can jump it off, and if you don't use the radio or lights you can probably get home, but it's not going to start in the morning," Clyde said as the thought of seeing her in the morning played in his mind. He continued, "I could go get my charger at the house, but eventually you are going to need a battery. If I go tonight, I can get you another one, and in the morning, you'll be ready to go."

"Oh, Mr. Stovall. You don't have to go to all that trouble. You've been really so kind to me just looking at it and…"

Clyde interrupted, "You have to go to work in the morning, don't you?"

"Yeah."

"Well, we need to get this fixed tonight."

Her warm smile of appreciation sealed the deal. She said, "I gotta get the kids at Ma Ma's though."

"Ok I'll follow you home and then run to town. The parts store closes at nine, I think."

On the drive Clyde thought of being with Jenny. He imagined the feel of her up against him. Callused hands on soft skin. His fantasy was suspended as he pulled up the creek-gravel drive of Jenny's grandmother's house. Just as he had told her, she left the car running when she went inside to get the kids. A few minutes later she came back without them.

"Savannah wants to spend the night, and Dylan went fishing." Jenny explained. As the ramifications sank in she added, "So it's just me and you tonight."

The two dropped off the car at her trailer, removed the faulty battery and rode to town in his truck. Her presence in the cab made Clyde's fantasies all the more palatable. And he noted how well she fit in there with him. *She fits better than this damn hat*, he thought. They arrived at the parts store four minutes after closing.

Clyde said, "Well, we can go to the super-store. Do you know your car's model year?"

"Uh, it's eight or nine years old?"

Even knowing the answer Clyde asked, "Did you buy it new?"

"No. We bought it used," Jenny said then regretted using "we." "We got everything used! And old!" she added with a laugh. Clyde laughed too.

Back at her place they chatted in the humid night air as he installed the battery. Gnats and moths were attracted to the work lamp. Other insects buzzed and clicked out in the dark yard. It was after ten by the time Clyde got the battery installed. "Can you come in for something to drink?" Jenny offered.

"Sure," Clyde said and turned toward her. Effortlessly, she slipped up close to him. Clyde involuntarily looked away. He clicked off the work light and drew a deep breath. In the starlit darkness, she took his left hand and placed it under her T-shirt. Tanned hands made their way to places the sun had not seen.

Clyde slept more soundly than he had in years. An hour later than usual he woke up at 5:00 a.m. Jenny was nestled next to him. His mind looked for ways to make it work. Without motion Jenny asked, "You ok?"

"Yeah." The sun was not up but already making its presence known. "But I need to go."

"Ok. I hope things are ok with us," she said.

"Yeah. It's ok. I gotta go." Clyde's mind raced ahead to the future both near and far. Nothing seemed the same, and he had no answers for the questions.

He dressed, all except his boots. Halfway across the living room he noticed Dylan eating cereal in the kitchen. *He must have just got here,* Clyde thought with a groan. There was an eternity of silence in that moment. Clyde frowned, ground his teeth and nodded somberly at the boy. The young man lifted his head back in acknowledgement. Clyde broke into a sweat on the front steps as he tied his boots. He couldn't get to the truck fast enough. And not before he heard the trailer door open behind him.

"Hey, Mr. Clyde you forgot your cap," Dylan said.

Clyde's blood ran cold. Embarrassed now, he turned around and took the hat. "Thanks."

"Yeah, no problem," Dylan said.

If Clyde could have teleported to his truck with a fifty-fifty chance of survival he would have taken it, but two steps from the cab, Dylan had one more thing to say, "You've been good to my mom." Clyde didn't believe it, but he nodded as he climbed in his truck.

#

A couple of weeks later, Inez Crabtree and her tablemates were sitting down for lunch at Mildred's. A widow for twenty-something years, Inez spent her time at church and going to any funeral, fund raiser, or community event she could attend. The conversation took on a softer volume as the women began to talk about Jenny.

"She sure is pretty. Shame about her husband," Laurice McGovern said.

"Yes, I heard he got a job in Scottsboro after getting fired at the mill," Munice Groce added. As they talked about his substance abuse problems, Inez fished her second pain pill of the day out of her purse. Jenny's figure, finances and future were bandied about. Of particular concern was her "overly friendly" ways with the farmers. The ladies had the good sense to time and regulate the tone of their conversation to minimize what others could overhear, yet none of them noticed when Clyde entered the building as usual for lunch.

Fields

Inez leaned over her plate and said, "Why, can't you just imagine her trying to hook her wagon onto one of these old tractors? Why, I could just imagine her and Clyde Stovall having an affair."

If she hadn't said his name Clyde probably never would have caught a thing, but his auditory memory recalled what he previously didn't hear.

He did hear how Inez continued.

"And poor Annie would never know. She hasn't left the house in months. Can't you just imagine what all has gone on in her life to make her so depressed?"

Clyde walked into their field of view and the women at the table tried to draw the words back from the atmosphere with a collective inhale. The new silence drew all the more attention to the surreptitious nature of the chatter. Wrinkled faces under meticulously-styled hair tracked his passing. Clyde's lips tightened and by habit he tipped his head in greeting and kept walking. Whispers rushed to fill the void after he passed. Clyde's thoughts also rushed.

#

The M Farmall popped and creaked its way to the shed as it had done for generations. The rain cloud had gathered friends and what started as a solo performance became a choir. The downpour washed the dust off the curved metal top of the tractor and pressed in on Clyde.

In spite of the deluge, his shaggy barn dog Leroy came out to greet him. The manifestation of loyalty played on chords of family, fields, and farming—a life well-lived not in its excitement but in its perseverance. Waves of anger and pain rose and fell as it dawned on

Clyde how resentful he had become of Annie. With Leroy plodding alongside, rain mixed with tears of forgiveness and repentance, and Clyde returned home from the fields once again.

--END--

Attention

Scott stared at his dog's water bowl. He could see the faintest tinge of red forming a ring. He didn't know if it was algae or mold. In his mind, something moved toward the surface, but his train of thought was interrupted by his mother's call.

"Scott! Scott? Where are you?

He tried to recapture the thought, but it was slipping away.

"Scott! I need you, Scott!"

"I'm coming, mother." Scott left the aborted notion and the water bowl in the same place and turned to his mother. She was propped up in the living room wedged into an oversized tan cloth recliner. She was oversized herself. Cans, dishes, papers, magazines and various remotes cluttered around her like orbital debris. "I need some more crackers. Go to the store for me. There is money in my purse, but bring me back my change. And don't be gone long."

Mindlessly, Scot shuffled through the purse for keys and cash. He would have completed his task, there and back, just as mindlessly, except when he opened the back door he tripped over the neighbor's cat. His mother called from the chair, "What's that?"

"Nothing, mom." Scott stared at the cat which had leapt off the stoop and watched him from between foundation shrubs.

"You ok, buddy? I didn't mean to step on you...I didn't see you."

"Pay attention!" came a sharp clear reply. Scott thought it was the cat. He looked across the yard at Mr. Brindley's house; it was his cat. A retired salesman, Mr. Brindley was a museum of all the things he used to sell. He was the kind of man who mowed his yard in plaid polyester trousers, old dress shoes and a wife-beater shirt. But Mr. Brindley was nowhere to be seen. Scott looked again at the cat. He didn't say anything else for fear the cat would say something back.

#

The clerk at Lentz's Cee Bee popped her gum as she rang up the box of Ritz crackers. "Five twenty-seven," she said. Pop. Pop. She turned her hand palm up with fingers curled to examine her nails. Scott fished for the cash, but his pockets were empty.

"Aaa," Scott uttered, "I can't...I can't find my money." His face grew warm. The embarrassment intensified when the clerk looked at him. He stared at the lattice of tattoos on her arm. Heavily mascaraed eyes blinked at him in silence.

"I guess I left it in the car," he stammered out.

Without hesitation, the cashier accepted the plan and said quite cheerfully, "Well, you can go get it." There was nobody else in line. There were only three other shoppers in the store. All were elderly folks passing the time. "I'll wait for you," she added.

"Uh. Ok," Scott said.

As he turned to go, another young man came striding through the automatic doors. A loose motorcycle jacket flapped around him like crows taking flight. His wavy black hair was enjoying its reprieve from the helmet in his right hand. "Hey, Janice!" he called to the clerk. She brightened immediately and smiled broadly, "Hey, Reggie honey!"

"I gotta get some stuff for lunch, babe," he said.

"Well, you know we got it."

Janice bit her lip as her eyes followed him out of sight down the first aisle. Scott watched her watching Reggie, and for the second time that day a thought struggled to surface. His phone rang. He pulled it out of his pocket and flipped it open, "Hello?" He knew Janice could tell it was a woman's voice on the other end, but he hoped she wouldn't be able to make out the words.

"Yes, mom. I'm here now. I'm almost done."

"Yeah ok. Give me a minute."

Scott closed the phone and lowered his eyes from Janice. Janice, whom he had seen two or three times a week for months, yet he never learned her name. He wished he had taken the call somewhere else. "My mom," he said, "It was her calling about the crackers." He noticed how the silver stud above her lip slid up when she smiled warmly at him. From somewhere in the back of the store, they heard Reggie, "Hey, Mr. Jamison!"

"I'll be right back," Scott said and hurried out the door to look for the money in the car. Obediently, the door opened when his foot struck the black rubber mat. Predictable and compliant just like it was made to be.

It was a bright summer day. The warm car felt good to Scott after being in the refrigerated air of the grocery. He sat in the driver's seat for a moment with eyes closed, letting the warmth soak into his bones. Muffled sounds of cars and people passing by added to the feeling of isolation. At first, he wasn't sure why tears slipped from his eyes, but the emotional note was sadness. Just plain sadness. Sadness for still living at home. Sadness for not being able to tell his mother "no." Sadness for not being Reggie and for not learning Janice's name.

Crap. Her name is Janice, and I've talked to her dozens of times and I've NEVER asked her name? What the hell is wrong with me? I'm a loser, that's what. It was the perpetual conclusion of any self-assessment. The summation of his existence and the terminus of any effort to change. His mind automatically started to reach for his mother's expectation, to find the money and get her the crackers, but the unspoken yet audible words of the cat came back: "Pay attention!"

What does that mean? Pay attention to what? He looked up at the rearview mirror to see himself. Unfashionably thick eyebrows shaded dark irises with bright whites. He stared into his own eyes, searching for something more than what he could see. The rising temperature brought him back and he began to look for the money. The extra effort and the heat produced a little sweat but no cash.

Fear subtly suggested he just drive home. And never come back. Instead he headed back into the store. The cooled air hit sharply on his damp face, but what really arrested him was seeing Reggie at the checkout counter. He was placing six bottled cokes, a small tube of bologna and some crackers on the black conveyor. He and Janice looked toward Scott as he approached.

"I can't find my money," Scott said plainly. "I don't know what I did with it."

"Oh," said Janice, "I've already rung up the sale. I'll have to back it out."

"Ok, sorry—" Scott started but Reggie interrupted, "Hey, man, I've got it."

"Huh?"

"No, don't worry, bro, I got it. See? I got the same taste in crackers," And Reginald tapped his box of Ritz. "Besides. I think I found your money. Was it a ten-dollar bill?"

"Uh, yeah," Scott nodded.

"Yeah, when I was coming in I saw this bill wrapped around the divider thingy." Reggie grinned, "I just thought it was my lucky day again." He smiled at Janice and she beamed back.

"So, here's your bucks, man. The luck is yours."

"Thanks," Scott said sincerely.

As Scott left the store, he could hear the clink of the bottles and Janice and Reggie's cheery chatter. "I'm gonna do that next time," Scott said to himself. "I will pay attention." And he did. When he opened the car door he noticed a ten-dollar bill fallen between the door and the seat as if someone had laid it there on purpose. He heard Reginald buzzing off on his motorcycle and turned to see him exit the parking lot with his lunch, wrapped in a brown paper bag, tied to the seat behind him.

Scott put the money in a different pocket than his mother's change. When the phone rang, he didn't answer it, and when he got home he washed the dog's water bowl.

--END--

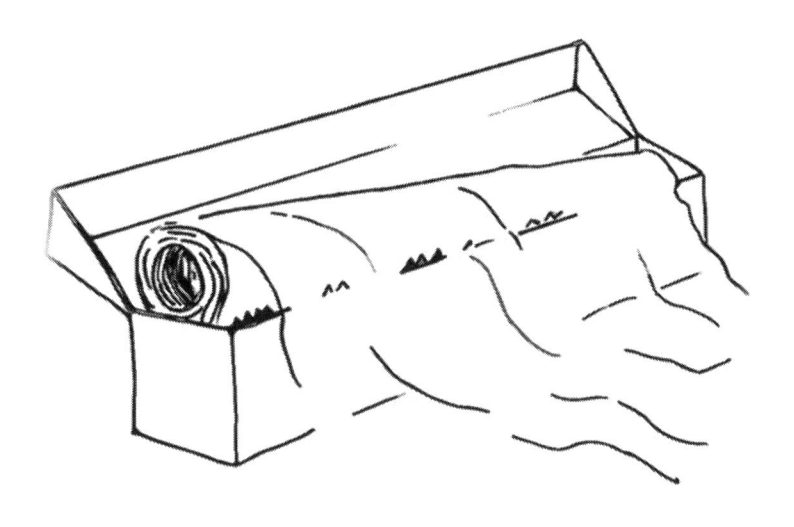

Liberation

The heavy-set man looked miserable carrying his two plastic grocery bags across the vast asphalt parking lot. The heels of his shoes were crushed flat where his feet rolled out. The cheap white tennis shoes matched the bags—both strained under the load. The shoes carried nearly three hundred and fifty pounds of flesh and the bags carried canned food. The fat man's feet kicked out in front of him like they were anxious for their turn to be out from under the burden.

It was the middle of the day and it was hot. The big man didn't notice when he stepped in someone's discarded gum. It had melted into the asphalt and rose up in stringy stickiness between the sole of his shoe and the pavement as he walked on unaware. Only a thin gritty residue remained by the time Greg got to his car.

A lean woman with frosted hair watched him from her car one aisle over. Cool air flowed from her dashboard, but it struggled against the sun's assault. Brenda watched the man labor toward his clunker. He was sweating and breathing heavily from the exertion. She felt sorry for him *Why, he's carrying around an extra man*, she thought. *I think he might need to be liberated.*

Greg's car lurched when he got in and it took a moment for the vehicle to find its level again. Brenda followed his car out of the parking lot. He turned right onto the highway and drove five miles per hour under the speed limit.

Greg didn't notice the Lexus trailing him. His mind was on getting home to the air conditioning. Heat like this aggravated his emphysema. He was sweating profusely and feeling disgusted with himself. "You fat pig," he said with a glance to the fifty-two-year-old man in the rear-view mirror. His right hand found its way into one of the grocery bags. He fumbled around for the Best Bakery box. Using his teeth, he pulled the box open and took out a pack of fudge-covered peanut butter wafers. The chocolate was already melting behind the cellophane. He had it eaten by the time he pulled into his driveway at 145 Westlawn Drive.

His house was a two-bedroom cottage with light gray hardboard siding and a black shingle roof. Greg had been a roofer and general construction worker until he injured his back. He lived alone since his wife had divorced him six years prior. He had tried to be mad at her, but he never could think of anything convincing to be angry at her about. "I wouldn't want to be married to me either," he had concluded.

He climbed the creaking steps up to the side door. At the top, he fumbled with the key while the swinging groceries pulled his hand away from the lock. The Lexus rolled silently by his property. He opened the door and felt the rush of chilled air. Stepping inside he took a deep breath and sighed.

Ten minutes and a dry shirt later Greg plopped into his recliner. As he reached for the remote, he heard someone rapping on his front door.

Brenda had learned a few things over all the years of helping people. One of the most important was not to arouse suspicion. Fortunately, most people were completely oblivious to their surroundings. But some people were "situationally aware" as the military put it.

That's why helping people in crowded places was especially risky. It simply increased the odds that someone would notice something out of the ordinary, but sometimes liberation required the risk. One time she had helped a homeless man out of his misery right in front of a convenience store.

She had seen him shuffling along the street toward the store. She quickly found a place to park and followed him for three blocks. That's why her car didn't show up on the surveillance camera. From the adjacent lot, she had watched him trade some wadded bills and several coins for an oversized bottle of beer. With his beer appropriately wrapped in brown paper, the bum exited the store, turned to his left and walked right toward her. She had moved to the evening shadows beyond the corner of the building. The place smelled of motor oil and vomit.

As he unscrewed the top of his beer and walked past an ancient ice machine she stepped directly in front of him. He looked up at her with his hand still on the cap like a kid caught in the cookie jar. When he saw her pretty smile of compassion, he smiled too. His broken teeth, weather-beaten skin and body odor confirmed she was doing the right thing.

Stepping forward, Brenda deftly placed her right leg behind his legs, brought her arm up across his chest, then slammed him backward onto the pavement. He weakly cried out as he hurtled toward the ground. She heard a satisfying crack when his head struck the concrete.

Quite to her surprise, the store clerk peeked his head out of the front door an instant later. He looked at her and then at the splayed man behind her on the ground.

Brenda calmly said, "He fell. Probably stone drunk. You better call an ambulance."

The clerk quickly nodded and ducked back inside. It was dark except for the street lights and bare fluorescent bulbs under the awning. The cheap lights of both competed to distort colors. The lamplights made whites orange and the fluorescents made them blue. Brenda could see a dark pool forming under the old man's head. Nearby, a wet paper bag discharged a foaming puddle of beer but pathetically retained the fragments of the brown bottle. Satisfied, she walked calmly back to her car.

The newspaper ran a tiny story on it. What made that rescue so amusing to her was how the store clerk described her to police: "A heavyset black woman." Of course, they didn't look too hard for her because she was just a witness to a fatal alcohol-induced fall of a homeless nobody.

Standing on the front steps of Greg's house Brenda told herself it was time to help another one. But things needed to fall in place first. She heard him grunt as he clambered out of the recliner. *Miserable? Check*, she thought.

Greg opened the door to an attractive professionally-dressed woman with a kind smile.

"Yeah?" he asked her. *Is she a lawyer?* he asked himself.

"Hi. I'm a realtor and wanted to know if I could ask you a few questions?" Brenda said. She could feel the conditioned air being drawn across her legs and into the humid heat. The room smelled of cooked onions and stale sweat.

Inclined to be agreeable, Greg agreed, "Uh ok."

"May I come inside?" she asked.

He hesitated for a moment, mostly out of concern for her sensibilities. She added, "I don't want to waste your air conditioning."

"Ok. Come in," Greg replied.

She stepped inside, pulling her purse off her shoulder and into her hands. She looked around at the ceilings, flooring and trim like she owned the place.

Greg closed the door and stood beside her. Several months of rubbish—drink cans, food wrappers and mail were piled on the room's horizontal surfaces. Brenda thought, *Passive, non-contributor? Check.* She didn't just free people from their misery; she freed society from the burden of carrying them.

"Nice old house this is. The high ceilings help to keep it cool, don't they?" Brenda asked.

"Yes. What did you say you wanted?"

"Well, like I said, I'm a realtor and I would like to learn a little bit about this neighborhood and this house. Depending on your answers I might be able to offer you the deal of a lifetime."

"I'm not really interested in selling. See, I've been living here—"

Brenda completed his sentence "—for a long time?"

He nodded. Her disapproving frown made Greg feel ashamed.

"Do you live here alone?"

"Yes," Greg said. *Check*, Brenda thought.

Starting with the age of the home and when he moved in, Brenda asked several real estate questions. She was, after all, a real estate agent. It never ceased to amaze her how much people would tell you if you could just get them answering questions. She found out Greg was divorced, disabled due to breathing problems, and had two grandchildren that lived seventy-four miles away. As far as she could tell, those two kids were the only thing that mattered to Greg.

Brenda wandered over to the kitchen thinking to herself, *So how do I answer the hopeless criteria? Certainly, there is almost no meaning to his life. Do those infrequent visits from the kiddies offset the fact that he has no health, no self-control and no ability to earn a living to support himself? I don't think so. Even if he retains some small emotion of hope he has nothing to give and nothing to look forward to. Hopeless? Check.*

She could see the white bag of canned goods sitting on the shelf. She had been inside long enough to realize that it was unusually cool. "You set the thermostat pretty low in here," she said.

"Yeah, it helps with my breathing." Greg was starting to get irritated. His legs ached and he wanted to sit down.

Brenda was assessing the last two criteria: privacy and opportunity. These had to do with her, not him. With her car parked behind a vacant "For Sale" house one street over and him basically living a hermit's life, she was confident she could do the deed without much risk of getting caught. *So, privacy?* she queried herself. *Check*, she gravely answered.

"Look, lady, I don't think I can help you. My house is not for sale. There's one around the corner that you can look at. It's for sale." Greg was nervous. He didn't want to offend her. And he didn't want her to think badly of him.

"What if I offered you $300,000 dollars?" Brenda asked still peering into the kitchen.

"What? I don't understand."

She turned around and looked at him, her purse strap back in place on her left shoulder, her right hand holding a .38 revolver out of his view behind her hip. "What if I paid you $300,000 for your house?" she said calmly.

"It's not worth that," Greg said.

"No, it's not, but would you make a deal if I paid you that?"

"I don't know. Why would you pay me that?"

"Double check on the passivity," Brenda said.

"What? What are you talking about?" Greg felt his face flush with aggravation.

Opportunity, or the means to execute the liberation, was always the ficklest of the criteria. Sure, she could shoot his fat ass, but obvious signs of murder created too much interest. She needed something more mundane. Besides, how to bring about a miserable human being's final escape was the part she relished the most about her ministry. It took discipline, creativity, and strength to release a person from their mortal hell, and she took pride in her abilities.

It turned out the box of plastic wrap sticking out of the grocery bag proved to be the spark of inspiration so she could say "Check" to the question of opportunity.

Greg realized something was wrong too late. And he was mistaken to think she was just there to taunt him.

"Look, lady, you got to leave," he said.

Brenda almost laughed out loud to see the color drain from his face when she leveled the pistol at him.

"Look, lady," Brenda mocked, "I will shoot you if you don't do exactly what I tell you. I will simply tell the police that you invited me over here with questions about listing your property, but then you attacked me and tried to rape me. I shot you in self-defense."

Greg had no doubt that she was capable of doing exactly that. He broke out in a different kind of sweat.

With the gun steadily trained on him, Brenda walked casually over to the counter and pulled out the plastic wrap. Within the bag, jars of spaghetti sauce and seasoned canned meat rolled around on the laminate countertop growling.

Brenda calmly lied, "Take this and wrap yourself up. When you are good and bound up I will get what I want and leave." She tossed the blue box at him.

Starting with his ankles Greg began to wind the plastic around his body. When his legs were secured she made him put his arms behind his back and she wrapped his hands and forearms. Then she made him stand and rotate. She spooled out the wrap as it wound around him. As she watched the clear, shiny plastic shroud his fat body, Brenda had her own moment of fear, *What if there is not enough in the roll to cover this fat slob?*

As he spun around, Greg wanted to cry. Absurdly, given his circumstances, a memory of gym showers in the ninth grade surfaced.

"Quick, call Greenpeace! A whale has washed up in the locker room!" Steven Hall's words were just as clear in Greg's mind as when he said them thirty-eight years prior. Others chimed in, "It's not a whale, it's the Pillsbury Doughboy!"

"Hey, don't insult the Doughboy! He ain't as fat as Prego Grego!" Greg wanted to crawl down the drain. That nickname would stick with him for years. At that moment, coach Reed, six foot tall and all tanned muscle stepped in. His voice boomed, "Hey knock it off in here! Derek! Steve! You get out of here. The rest of you too."

Greg's own father had never been involved enough to help Greg, much less rescue him, but in that moment Greg was flooded with relief and gratitude for Coach Reed.

"Thanks, Coach," he said sincerely, "I didn't know what to do." The words pushed out tears.

"Well, you could lose some weight, blubber boy, and they wouldn't harass you."

Something died that day in Greg, maybe ambition or confidence. Maybe hope. Greg was jerked out of his memory when "the crazy lady with the gun" yelled, "That's enough!"

#

He stood in the center of the living room floor like a bloated Oscar. Only his head could move. It was hard to breath. The crazy lady studied him like he was a fish in the butcher's display case. She walked around. Satisfied he couldn't move, she put the gun back in her purse and put the purse on the kitchen table.

Greg's hair stood on end when she pulled out a small pen knife from her purse. She cut the wrap free from the roll. She then calmly walked over to him and shoved him viciously backward. He fell like a log and rattled the entire house. He struggled to regain his breath while she started to wind more wrap under the soles of his feet and up behind his neck pulling his knees up toward his chest. She was compressing him. After he suffocated she planned to remove the wrap and leave.

Greg realized he was going to die. As the crazy woman frantically cocooned him, a strange terror iced every cell of his body. It wasn't the fear of death, but of the undeniable recognition that he had not lived.

He could say he was content with his construction jobs, but he knew he never did more than asked. He had told himself that he had deferred every decision to his wife so she could have what she wanted, but the dawning of death proved that he was just indifferent. He wanted to pretend that being a good father was never getting angry, but all he had done was convince his kids that he didn't care.

Like a spider hovering over him, Brenda worked furiously to complete the job. Flat on his back with his knees pressed up to his chest and his face pulled down by the ever-tightening wrap, Greg found it harder and harder to breath. His lungs burned and his heart thundered inside his ribcage. He looked up at his killer. Her hair hung around her head like a cloud and her face was contorted into a demonic expression of hatred. Sweat dripped from the tip of her nose into Greg's eye and it stung sharply.

Blinking away the burn Greg saw the two small photos of his grandchildren hanging on the wall behind her. Lucy and Daniel. School photos from three years ago. They were both in middle school now. Greg had loved them like he had loved everybody else—passively.

He was there when they came to visit. He went to some events when invited. He didn't ask. He didn't invite or initiate. He didn't intrude and he wasn't involved. *I've never done a damn thing for either one of them,* Greg thought. Emotions familiar and new swirled within him: regret, anger, shame, desire, and defeat. But the familiar tears of hopelessness were absent.

Something obvious but previously invisible because it had never been considered occurred to Greg as he lay on his back gasping for breath. Namely, that he had been in weight training all his life because of his obesity. Carrying around three hundred and fifty pounds makes for stout legs and Greg decided to use them to shove her off him. He pushed, but the plastic restrained him.

The effort made the world gray around the edges. He gulped for air and pushed again and felt something slip. Then he blacked out.

He felt a vicious slap on his left cheek and a spray of spittle on his face. His killer was leaning over on his feet pushing her weight down into him.

"Die already, you fat worthless slob!" she screamed.

As she bore down with his feet against her torso, Greg's knees were pushed ever so slightly out, creating some slack in the loop around his feet and neck. His face was blood red and he was dripping with sweat. He could no longer breathe. With one last titanic effort, Greg overcame forty years of inertia and launched the skinny murderous real estate lady across the room. She smashed into the door jamb around the front entry and collapsed to the hardwood. The photos of his grandkids rattled to the floor.

Her pen knife rotated weightlessly in the air above him for a moment before burying its two-inch blade into his abdomen. It didn't hurt. In fact, it looked amusing to see the rounded stainless-steel handle rising out of his belly like a knight in shining armor standing alone on the crest of a hill. Desperate for air Greg rolled on his left side and struggled to loosen the wrap around his forearms. Blackness approached and receded. His hands were numb and all he could move were his shoulders. Blood from his stomach trickled under the wrapping and puddled underneath him.

He could hear his assailant groaning and starting to come to. With another heave, he slipped his right arm free from the bit of wrap on his wrists. His whole body was still tightly wrapped, but the blood, sweat and stretching of the plastic allowed him just enough slack to move his arm, still inside the wrap, to the front of his body. He mashed his stomach in so he could pull the knife out and into his grasp. There was not enough clearance so Greg had to cut a three-inch incision into his own stomach to get the blade free. Unlike the puncture, the cut hurt like hell.

The woman started to crawl feebly toward her purse. Greg remembered the gun. There was no time to cut himself free. He needed minutes, but there were only moments. He yelled in frustration. She, or the devil inside her, laughed. The thought of making it this far only to die anyway was intolerable. Old lessons of incompetence and failure tried to shift him back into neutral. Part of him, like a rabbit in an eagle's claws, just wanted to surrender and accept his fate. Instead he did the only thing he could do—he started to roll toward her. At first she was perpendicular to his body, but as he rolled he pivoted parallel to her. She tried to army crawl past him. Then all three hundred and fifty pounds of Greg Lassiter rolled on top of his would-be murderer.

It was satisfying to hear the air rush out of her lungs and feel her bones between his body and the hardwood floor. She was face down with her arm pinned under her body and across her chest. Like a bloated silver caterpillar, Greg squirmed up on top of her. With his back on her back, he felt/heard her shoulder pop out of socket. She squealed in pain. He giggled as she struggled weakly under him, Greg used the knife to cut himself free from the food wrap. Ten minutes and a lot of sawing later, he was liberated.

--END--

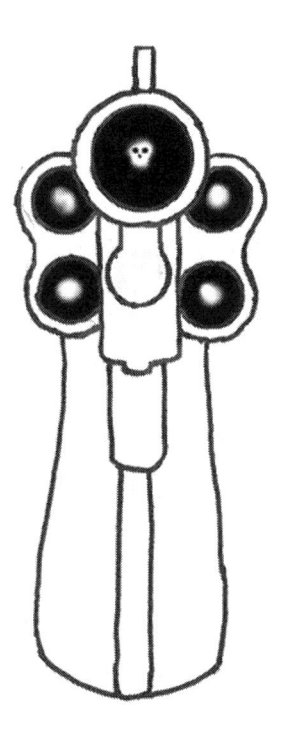

Last

I try not to think about the unchangeable past or the hopeless future so I wind up thinking a lot about myself. For example, I've given way too much attention to what I want for Christmas. I guess it's pretty selfish, but then nobody else is going to get me anything. The Christmas gift is a challenge because I literally own everything. I can take whatever I want and there's no one to complain. But don't get me wrong or think I'm a thief; it's just that as far as I can tell, I'm the last man on earth.

It's been over a year since it, whatever it was, happened. Two years ago, I didn't think about anything except what I was doing at the moment, and now I actually think about how I think. There's reason to think I'm crazy. However, what I've been through would make anyone crazy.

"Ain't that right?" I say to Stemmy, my gray matter.

"Yes, it is." Stemmy, despite being my imaginary companion, always speaks in the best English. He's mostly concerned with practical things, but sometimes ol' Stem surprises me.

"Like right now; you need to get us back inside," says Stemmy.

"Yeah, you are right of course."

It's December 20th and the afternoon is drawing dark. The climate may be changing, but daylight still gets short in winter.

"Nobody has any Christmas lights out this year," I say as I walk out of the supermarket with a tub of groceries.

"They never do," Stem observes.

"People just don't have that Christmas spirit like they used to."

I strap the groceries to the back of my motorcycle and head home. Home is a well-built house in Murfreesboro in a fine neighborhood. I settled there for the winter in part because it took me hours to break inside. I figured if it was that much of a challenge for me then it would also be difficult for others, human or animal. Stem approved.

By the way, Stem's full name is Sir Stemical Gray Matter. He doesn't like it when I call him that because he says it is inaccurate. I tell him he can find someplace else to live if my skull doesn't suit him. He never laughs.

Four Hundred Three, Rochester Lane is a lot of house for one man. Two stories, a full basement, propane generator and a fallout shelter. It came well stocked with ammunition, food, and a water purification system preinstalled. It was the Williamses that lived here before.

"Williams is preferred," Stem advises.

"Well, the Williams left us a fine set up and even spared us the inconvenience of having to remove their corpses," which is often the case with the homes I inherited. Sometimes, it isn't even a whole body but whatever scraps are left after rats and coyotes get through.

The sky is graying blue and the traffic, as always, is at a standstill. I weave my way through the jumble as I think about what to get myself for Christmas again.

Breaking with my better judgment to avoid the past, I say to Stem, "The first few months were the worst, weren't they? Sometimes you could smell that there was bodies inside—"

"You mean to say, 'Sometimes you could tell that there were bodies inside by the odor.'" Sir Stem corrects.

"Don't cut me off," I reply but he's ignoring me. He always ignores me when I'm right. "It's not polite to interrupt, Mr. Matter."

"You are, of course, correct, Nathaniel. I apologize."

Anyway, as I was saying, the Williams were not at home when…when it happened. So I didn't have to remove their bodies. They seem to have been fine folks. Papers around the house make me think Mr. Williams was a doctor or somebody who worked for a hospital. I have more papers to go through. Maybe he was an attorney.

"Now Mrs. Williams. She is a real looker. Ain't she Stem?"

"Yes, she was quite attractive."

I left most of the family photos undisturbed, but the ones with her I added to the walls in the bunker. Now don't feel sorry for me that I sleep in a bunker. It's not that bad. Maybe twenty by twenty with a steel door and its own filtered ventilation system. It was a bitch getting the mattress down in there, but Stem sleeps better in the comfort of concrete.

"Technically, I don't sleep. It's just—"

"It's just that I lose consciousness."

"Correct."

I go to the front door when we get home, because other than one of the garage doors, the rest are barricaded. I hated to park the German sedan out on the street, but the Hummer is about survival so it gets to stay inside. Before everybody died, I never thought about survival at all. Now, I swear, it's calling the shots on everything I do. The locks click open, and out of habit I enter looking-listening for my friend. No one greets me.

"Rex is no longer with us." Stem says.

"Yes. I know Rex is no longer with us." My words turn into a puff of vapor in the cold house.

Rex is a German Shepherd. I found him soon after it happened. It was pretty bad on me when everybody up and died, but it was even worse on the pets that survived. Birds dying in cages. Cats locked inside. I've avoided going to any zoos. And then there were the dogs. Penned or chained until they died of thirst or starved because there wasn't any people.

Stem corrects my grammar, "'Because there weren't any people.'"

"Shut up, Stem." I pull out my flashlight and go to the kitchen to fix supper. Rex and I would eat the same things. His first meal with me was a bag of cheese curls and some jerky. Unlike the other dogs I rescued, Rex stayed with me. Maybe it was the cheese curls.

Waking up to a world where everybody is dead is kind of hard on you. I can't say what happened because I don't know. It was just me moving and everyone else dead. Bodies are just laid out on the streets or wherever. Lots of bodies in stores, and I never, ever, ever want to go into another high-rise building. I've avoided schools too. Churches are ok.

At first, I kept feeling like it was a dream, but I kept living and eating, sleeping and shitting, and nobody takes a dump in a dream. Alarms and fires slowly died down. I started rescuing animals or at least releasing them. That's when I noticed most of the larger animals died, too. I haven't seen a living horse or cow. I knew I couldn't save them all, but like the boy throwing starfish back in the sea, I thought I could make a difference to some of them.

That's how I found Rex. He was penned on the back side of a collision repair center, Jumby's Paint and Auto Body Shop. I guess he was a guard dog. It was September three days after. I'd been to a sporting goods store for guns and gear. I saw Rex inside the chain-link pen as I was coming down the street on my bike.

Jumby's doors were wide open and a whiff of death slid by as I made my way to the back. The bright morning light glinted off the new chain-link fencing. Rex sat motionless watching me approach. I could see where he had tried to dig through the concrete to escape. The gate had a padlock. Some dogs growled and snapped but Rex was a silent fur statue.

I found Jumby bloated and oozing on the shop's floor. Fortunately, he kept his keys on a loop. If I'd had to dig through his pockets he would have burst. Rex stood when he heard the jingle of the keys but didn't make a sound. His silence kinda creeped me out actually. I found the right key on the second try and backed away pistol in hand. I'd actually had to shoot a couple of dogs. Nothing is worse than having to kill something when everything is already dead.

"You did what you had to do."

"Yes, Stem. Thank you."

Rex didn't run out or run off. He just walked slowly toward me as if his wet nose was pulling the rest of him. I took out some beef jerky, and he devoured it. Next were the cheese curls. Not a one hit the ground.

"Water! You need water," was the first thing I ever said to him. It would be a while before he ever said anything to me.

I turn on my little lantern and fix my supper. You can get just about anything you care to eat in a can, but I miss steak. I do grill the occasional squirrel or rabbit, and it's growing on me but sometimes the flavor and chew of a good T-bone haunts me.

At first, I guess I was just in shock. It all seemed unreal. There was power in some places for weeks so I would turn on TVs and radios, but it was static or error messages or automatic programming. Cell phones seemed to work, but no one ever answered.

Then it occurred to me that the apocalypse could be a local thing. Talk about denial. I went to the Atlanta Hummer dealership and picked up a new H4-MAX, loaded it with supplies and extra gas and headed east then north. People had died suddenly, instantly really, and the roads were stopped up with vehicles. Still interstate medians and shoulders were the clearest routes. I figured I averaged twenty miles an hour. For weeks, I'd travel until my tank was half empty then pull over, look around for signs of life in whatever town or area I was in and then move on. Despair like a tumor gathering mass grew in me, but Rex helped.

Gasoline was hit or miss. Sometimes pumps would work, if I could find a backup generator and sometimes not. I could always siphon it from cars but they would be empty if they'd been running when It happened. I got to where I just looked for a corpse inside before I even tried. Truck stops were the best bet. The pumps might work, and if not, the parked cars gave the next option. The big rigs made me think about switching to diesel.

Rex and I had been on the road for a few weeks when I rolled up under the still lighted awning of a Jet-Way in Virginia for a resupply. It was late fall and raining like heaven was trying to drown us. "Out Rex." He followed me out of my door and sniffed the ground and then the air. I could hear the generator running. I went to the pump. It was on but like always, prepay only. I grabbed my shotgun. By then Rex knew the routine.

Some buildings caught on fire after, but there was no sign of fire here. Inside, bodies were slumped in booths and spilled out in the floor like oversized stuffed toys. The smell was always bad—and the flies. I held my nose in my shirt and started messing with the pump controls behind the register.

That's when Rex spoke to me for the first time. It was a clear sharp bark. I looked over the counter. His head was down and facing the drink coolers on the back wall. The low growl from him raised both my hair and my gun. The ceiling light flickered in that corner as if darkness was trying to strangle it.

"Hello? Is anybody there?" I called.

There was a rustle, and Rex crouched lower. I stepped from behind the counter keeping my pistol grip shotgun aimed at the back. "If you are a person I'm not going to hurt you but if you—" then I saw three or four of them. "Coyotes!" I shouted. The canines scrambled clickitty-clack across the tile floor toward us. I drew a bead on the lead and blasted him. The roar of the gun was deafening, but the rest kept coming. By the time I racked another shell the second was almost atop Rex. Boom! Came the report and it fell aside. A third came at me and a fourth lunged at Rex who met his opponent mid-air.

With the gun I struck at the tawny beast attacking me, but the glancing blow was little more than a distraction. Dark pools of liquid fury glared at me from above snapping teeth. It leapt for my throat while I tried to rack another shell. It was faster. Instinctively, I raised my left arm and its jaws clamped down. I felt little pain but immediately couldn't move my arm for the weight and pressure. We tumbled to the ground, and I panicked. The image of the vicious animal ripping my face off immobilized any offensive efforts.

Rex, however, good old Rex, was my savior.

"You make too much of that dog." Stem says coldly.

"The hell I do. He saved my ass and you too!" The Williams's empty house swallows the sound, and I remember I am alone, "Rex was a great friend and you shut the hell up about him."

Rex had crushed his own attacker. I lay on my back with mine on top of me jerking my arm back and forth as if to rip it off. I felt the collision as Rex launched himself teeth first at the coyote forcing it to let me go. The two wrestled, snapped and rolled around and I scrambled to my feet looking for a clean shot. A moment of separation came where wild and domestic stood face to face. I stepped up next to Rex and the coyote fled.

Its teeth did not puncture my Kevlar jacket, thank God, but my arm was bruised as hell. Poor Rex's ears were bleeding. I guess from the shotgun. My own ears hummed for days after. Note to self: Do not discharge a firearm indoors.

"Unless your life depends on it." Stem chimes in.

Rex and I continued our quest for the living for weeks. We stopped at small towns, cities and farm houses. Eventually, the metal tombs on the Interstate were evidence enough that Rex and I should keep moving. I looped up the East coast, stopping short of Washington; I'm not sure why. Then we headed west.

Things got bad for me in December. The matter-of-fact optimism that comes from doing something gave way to reality. More and more, I struggled to see any point in living. I looked beneath my feet and only saw bottomless depths of meaninglessness.

We settled at Salt Fork State Park in Ohio for the winter. The resort kitchen had plenty of food supplies and gas stoves. The lake gave us a place to fish. The second day there, Rex found love or at least a bitch in heat—another Shepherd. She stood at the edge of the woods and totally captivated Rex.

"You want to go out? I asked. He just stared. "Rex, you want to go spend some time with a lady friend?" He whimpered at that. "Rex, Rex!" brought his eyes to me and I said, "Go!" and he took off like a shot. I felt some better letting him run loose. Survival of the species, right? He came dragging in exhausted a couple of days later. I tried to make the best of our new surroundings, but short days and more time inside made the depression deepen and darken.

I tried to read, but on the other side of bored is a desert without concentration. The lake was a pristine postcard of silver blue reflections ringed with dark evergreen trees. Most of our time was spent indoors, but we would go fishing. Rex's girlfriend would come around but never close and never onto the frozen lake.

As the lake started to freeze from the edges it pretty much eliminated fishing from the shore. My mind caught that image of slowly dying from the outside in. That's when I realized it makes no difference whether I live or not.

"It matters to me," Stem interjects. I clean up the kitchen and carry my dinner downstairs with tonight's movie.

"Yes, but you were not around then. Remember? At least you weren't talking anyway."

I close the steel door behind me and flip the switch for the generator. Outside the propane-powered machine begins to run, and my room warms with light. I strip and eat my supper in bed. The movie is about a racecar driver winning races and losing his girlfriend. It's dull, but maybe it's because I don't have a racecar or a girlfriend.

"Of course, I could get a racecar," I say. "For Christmas."

"There is no reason for you to get a racecar," Sir Stem counsels.

"Yeah, but there is no reason not to."

"Just that you could kill us all."

"Would it matter?"

"Yes, it matters!"

"How does it matter? Tell me that Sir Stemical. How does it matter?"

"It matters if you live or die."

"It matters to you. But to me it does not matter. I can get a racecar or not, but I will never ever have a girlfriend, or any kind of friend."

"You always get this way in winter."

"Yeah, because I've got time to think about how pointless it is. The rest of the time I'm just fooling myself."

"You should get a porno next time."

"Are you out of your mind? Or rather are you out of MY mind? That's enough."

I turn off the TV and take a revolver from my makeshift night stand. It's heavy in my hands. The polished steel shows craftsmanship. When everything is yours for the taking, you can afford the best. Would the men and women who made it mind if I use it to blow out my brains?

Stem wordlessly reminds me of the last time I attempted suicide. It was at Salt Fork last January, and it was a disaster. We had been there a couple of months, and the lake had frozen almost all the way over. I had found a little rolling fishing hut at the resort and had taken up ice fishing. It gave me and Rex something to do even though he never felt comfortable on the ice.

The shed was little bigger than an outhouse, and being from the South, I was more familiar with an outhouse than a fishing house. I had a padded stool and Rex would nap on a thick yoga mat.

The day was January 23rd —my birthday. It had snowed heavily the night before which made our walk to the fish house something of an effort. I imagined us as little figurines on a giant birthday cake. Frosting, cold and sweet, clumped on the evergreens and blanketed the expanse of the lake except for the ice-water channel in the middle. Maybe it was the birds-eye perspective but for the first time since it happened I thought about God.

God seems a terror to me. An interloper that cannot be contained. Bring God into the picture and everything gets distorted.

"That's why we don't need him," Stem offers.

By definition, a divine being would have to extend far beyond our limited comprehension, and if that is the case, what is the point in thinking about God?

There is no reason to think about what you can't comprehend but then people do. And I guess more so when death lurks.

Rex slept at my feet. He could probably survive without me, but he would survive better with me. Maybe that was the role of God. To assist with survival. Of course given what happened, it didn't seem God could be that concerned with human survival or perhaps lacked the power to ensure it.

I had the door of the shed open and facing the far shore with the northwest wind to our back. Cold, silent and impossibly smooth, the lake looked like the end of the world. I knew in my bones that I could accomplish nothing that made any difference. The tracks of our passing would soon enough be covered as the Earth turned 'round, mindless of the bits of flesh scrambling over her face. Eons will pass and the earth herself will be consumed by her sun turned red. Then what? Then back to dust and space. Irrelevant specks of nothingness scattered across a void.

The image of water under me captivated my darkened mind. Just a few inches of ice between me and that oblivion seemed like a kind invitation. As quietly as possible, I stood up to do what I should have done the day after it happened.

Rex, ever watchful, awoke anyway. At the doorway, I turned back to face him. "Stay," was my command. He lowered his head in obedience.

The shelter of the shack seemed insignificant until I came out into the wind. The dry cold sought every crack in my cover and sucked heat from me as a chimney draws smoke. I veered to the right to be out of Rex's line of sight and headed toward the open water.

Freezing to death at the bottom of a lake seemed a fitting end to the last man on earth.

As I approached the open channel the ice popped and cracked. I didn't want to fall partially through so I walked slowly and carefully. The water was transparent blue and passing silently by. Then I heard Rex call me. I turned back to see him standing in that stately posture that is natural for his breed, and he was looking my way. He barked again.

"Stay!" I shout but the distance and wind steals the words. Then he starts toward me. The decision to die solidifies in my mind and it must happen before Rex arrives to stop me! I run clumsily through the snow toward the water. The snow is thinner here and so is the ice. Before I reach the clear blue, the ice shelf gives way and I plunge down a hole big enough for my legs but not my chest.

Sharp knives stab my legs without mercy. It's so physical I actually believe pike are biting me. I struggle to drop further down, but the bulk of my coat forms a wedge. Then Rex is upon me tugging my collar. As strong as he is, he's not strong enough to pull me out. Instead of a living hell or an icy death, my choice is now to fight his efforts or cooperate. For him. For Rex, I cooperate. I push up against the ice and kick my legs—thick and heavy as wooden planks.

Rex pivots around to face me. I give my arm and he pulls me out. I feel like I have been crushed from my chest down. Even the snow feels warm.

Rex is barking at me. I imagine him saying, "You idiot! What are you doing? What the hell are you doing?"

I love him. Then like a trap door the ice beneath him gives way.

"Oh my God!" I scramble toward him on my stomach, but he's not in a hole. The entire section has given way and he's in the water floating away.

"Rex! Rex!" I follow along beside, but we are never close enough for me to grab him. I think to jump in for him, but then he would have no hope to survive.

"I didn't want this, Rex! I didn't want this!"

I see a small protrusion into the channel and scramble to it. I lay out flat reaching as he floats by. My hand dips into icy death and then a handful of fur. Just enough! I pull him back atop the ice. His eyes are bright, but he lays there breathing heavy.

Careful of the thin ice, I pick him up and run back. There is a small heater but no blankets in the shed. My legs and my heart burn as I carry him inside the resort. Somewhere along the way, my friend, my only friend, dies.

Two days later Stem shows up.

"It's not your fault," he said.

I didn't know how to respond, but I knew it wasn't true.

"You did what you had to do."

I didn't argue. It takes effort to argue and there was nothing left in me. Over the next few weeks Stem would speak up as clear as a bell and gradually I began to respond. I guess that means I'm officially insane. Not only hearing voices but talking back!

Now, I'm sitting here in my concrete bedroom with the weight of suicidal madness and this beautiful revolver bearing down on me. It could have been a Christmas gift for someone. I hear suicides increase around the holidays.

"Put the gun away," Stem says.

I look at the painting of Mrs. Williams. Her long legs crossed elegantly as she sits upright on one of the leather chairs from upstairs. She is stately and noble and at her feet is her dog, a black Lab named Stezer. He's dead in the pen behind the house and fine Mrs. Williams is dead somewhere else.

My mind halfheartedly gropes for a reason not to join them in that deep. The flotsam makes the swim all the harder—everyone is gone, Rex is gone, my mind is gone. This is why it's pointless to think about it. I am powerless to undo the past or change anything that matters. The waters wait.

With a concussive click, hopelessness settles into place, and it brings some clarity. I put the revolver down, and I get up in the morning. I pack my gear and set the house up for extended vacancy. I don't know when, or if, I'll be back.

"What do you mean, you don't know?"

I refuse to answer. It doesn't take me long to pack. I leave by 9:00 a.m. and head north in the Hummer. I take the 840 loop and head east on I-40.

"Where are we going?"

It's hard not to answer back, but I'm done.

"You're going back to Salt Fork, aren't you? You are going back to kill yourself. It's that dog, isn't it? You can't get over that dog."

The miles unravel in silence.

I've been on the road three days. I'm tired of sleeping in the vehicle. Stem has been fairly silent except for my dreams. Last night I had a nightmare that Rex and I were crossing a river only to get swept away in the rushing current. I was fighting for my life but just as panicked to see Rex getting pulled away by the brutal waters.

Then Stem showed up. He was sixty feet tall—a smooth alabaster-stone giant. He looked down at me and laughed. His hollow chest echoed the sound. Stiffly he reached down and pulled me from the river. He carried me off, lumbering across the countryside. My eyes strained to find Rex in the river, and I woke up screaming his name.

"You're better off without that dog."

I loathe Stem now, but I can't get rid of him. Audio books from Cracker Barrel help, and I continue north. I'm not exactly sure what for. Maybe Stem is right.

On Christmas Eve morn, I arrive at the park. It's just as I left it. I have to look away from the pallet I made for Rex in the kitchen. The snow on the partially covered lake makes it impossibly bright, but that's not the reason I don't look. Christmas morning dawns cold and clear. I suit up in the same gear as last time and head toward the lake.

I've kept it hidden from myself, but the suicidal impulse is here. I walk out on the ice. It's not near as extensive or thick as it was last time but the inviting oblivion under my feet is the same. Stem is silent. Perhaps I've heard the last of him.

And good riddance! That ass didn't love Rex.

The sky is blue and cold. I walk forward with eyes closed. The loudest sounds are my boots crunching through crusty snow. I filter out my steps to hear the breeze. Trees rustle. The scent of the evergreens comes to me. Soon, as I walk slowly out, I hear the water ripple and make its little splashes. It's like the applause of fairies urging me on. I smell the water now and feel tiny crackles in the ice with each step.

If ever Stem is going to speak up it is now, but what I hear next is yipping. Some sharper and others more raspy. I look back toward the tree-lined shore, where limestone rocks form ledges on the slope down, and I see them—probably half a dozen puppies on the eastern shore. In the shadows of the evergreens, Rex's lady friend watches over her brood and out at me. The largest pup is five feet out on the ice barking at the fool that I am ... just like his father.

The cold air bites at the tears in my eyes. Stem, if he's even there, doesn't say a word.

--END--

Riverside

The river water smelled of fish and algae, and lapped splish-splash against the pylons of the wooden dock. The waves rocked the fiberglass boat hull against its hold making hollow knocking sounds. Marly made her way to the end. Her tanned feet, toughened by the summer, padded quietly across the weathered planks. It was after midnight and the moon, like a half-eaten biscuit, crumbled its light atop the ripples of the river. With vacationers and summer residents bedded down for the night, the loudest sound was the buzz of amorous crickets and frogs. Laughter and unintelligible vocalizations from a distant and drunken bonfire came across the water to her like someone else's mail.

Moments before, Marly had slipped quietly out of her aunt and uncle's house, leaving her younger sister Abby sleeping peacefully in the guest room. Only a few days before, their parents had told them that they were divorcing. The stay with Aunt Ginny and her husband Rick was the consolation prize. Marly couldn't sleep; her mind kept replaying parts of that conversation.

It had begun with the phrase, "We are getting a divorce..." and she missed most of what they said after as those words floated around in her head. It sounded so calm and ordinary as if "getting a divorce" was like getting a gallon of milk or soap: "Hey, honey I'm going to town. I'll get us a movie and a divorce." By the time she was able to tune back in her mom was saying, "You

two are going to get to spend a couple of weeks at Aunt Ginny's."
What? Marly asked herself. Who does that? But she didn't have an answer.
She knew they argued and could see for herself the change in affection—the absence of something sweet rather than the presence of something bad—but what she struggled to attain was a vision of her life after "a divorce." That fuzzy future stymied her. The midnight dock seemed a good place to sort through things since no one wanted to talk about it. Her sleeveless pajama top with matching shorts were little protection from the cool night air, but with intensity of purpose and unspoken anger, her twelve-year-old body adjusted.

#

"You know they are going to split up," Marly had said to Abby while they waited for their mother to pick them up after dance some months back—even before the divorce announcement.
Abby ignored the unwelcome assertion.
Marly tried to make it more of a conversation instead of a confrontation; "I'm just saying, don't you know how they don't get along and act like it's a chore to be together?"
Still no takers.
"Mom acts mad all the time and dad just stays gone. Even when he's home, he's not really there."
Abby adjusted her backpack and looked down the street as a castaway might scan the horizon; "Abby, I'm not trying to be mean; I just want you to know what's going on."

"Look!" Abby's voice soared, "It's mom!" but by the time she took two steps toward the curb she realized it wasn't her mother's car.

Marly put her arm around her little sister and the eight-year-old cried soft tears into her side.

#

Aunt Ginny was her mother's sister and had a lake house instead of children. She loved Marly and Abby like only fun-loving aunts can do. Uncle Rick went along and was nice enough, but the bond was shared with the ladies. Time at the lake house had always been a special treat.

The moonlight silvered the already gray dock. Marly stood and let her toes hang over the edge. She noted how naturally and strongly they curled down as if to grip the wood for a lunge into the dark water. It occurred to her that the same force was always at play when she was standing, but only a ledge revealed it. She reminded herself why she was outside in the middle of the night with an overheard conversation between Aunt Ginny and her mother.

"I just don't think I can do this anymore," Marly had heard her mother say. Marly was supposed to be in bed then too. Instead, she was sitting on the floor with her back against the wall under the porch windows. Her mother was outside on her cell phone and sitting on the porch swing. She didn't swing, but it creaked anyway.

"He's not gonna change. I've asked him to see a counselor, but he's so stubborn and such a know-it-all. Now I don't even want it myself anymore." Marly couldn't make out her aunt's response and so intensely wished to hear. If anyone knew what to say, it was Aunt Ginny.

"Yeah, I know but you don't know what it's like," was her mother's irritated reply. "You've got Rick and he's never cheated on you so you don't really know how it is here…" Marly knew enough about love and sex to have some comprehension of what cheating meant. Her mind went back and forth between trying to figure out if the accusation was true and calling up visages of women it might be.

Her dad was affectionate and helpful when help was needed, but his emotions were a mystery to her. Like the water under her feet, she knew there was more below the surface but had no way to see. The dock was on one side of a small inlet. Four other houses ringed it also. The Tennessee River was flat and broad and seemed to not be moving at all unless some bit of trash or driftwood revealed its current. In the dark, Marly couldn't see the far side but knew from ski boat sightseeing that it was a wooded bank with nicer houses than her aunt's.

She had a sudden notion to dive into the liquid darkness to either plumb its depth, or surface and swim to the other side. In her fantasy, she swam and swam—deep and cold and exhausting. Instead she sat down and let her feet dangle. She had to point her toes down to reach the water. It was warm.

#

"What the hell is wrong?" Marly's father had shouted as her mother bustled her toward the park's picnic table. This was years ago, before Abby was even born, and Marly had cut her foot on a glass bottle half buried in the playground sand.

Her mother brushed past him, almost knocking the can of beer from his hand. The sloshed beer foamed its protest. Marly looked at him with tear-filled eyes and he followed. With sharp angry movements, her mother began to gather materials to clean the wound.

"Can I look at it, honey?" her dad asked gently and he squatted down for a closer view. Marly was frightened by the cut and the blood and more scared that her parents might do something to cause even more pain. "It's ok. I'm not going to hurt you," her father said.

"Move," her mother said to him. Marly wouldn't have known how to describe it, but she saw clearly the contempt on their faces. She needed seven stitches. The stitches didn't help it feel better.

Marly laid back on the dock and recalled other memories of their interactions. Not all of it was bad—the vacations to Six Flags, some holidays—but there was always distance and disagreement. Like the planks under her back, the family was both her support and the most uncomfortable thing in her life. With no one to talk with, the emotions often overwhelmed Marly. She had been hoping to talk with her aunt, but the time had not come up; or more likely Aunt Ginny kept things innocuous because she knew Abby didn't want to discuss anything.

She had tried to pray, but God went best with church, and as the marriage disintegrated, their erratic attendance seemed to Marly to set God far away. She looked up to the moon, brighter on her eyes than the glow it cast on the earth. *So, now what?* she prayed. The night sounds were quieter, and she listened. Even the revelers had settled down. Out over the channel, moon-cloud shadows moved; she couldn't tell if they were retreating or advancing.

She spoke out loud, "I don't know how to do this, don't you know." It wasn't a question but some followed: "What are people going to think or say? When will it happen? Why? Who are we gonna live with?" She paused to consider the variations, then continued with growing resentment. "So, if they can stop loving each other, can they stop loving us? Why didn't You help them stay together? Why didn't You do something?" The whys came in a bitter rush, but the raw emotion felt satisfying. When she ran out of words and accusations a deep sadness, a wordless grief, flooded her. Tears ran down her temples into her ears.

Unexpectedly, off and to her left, she heard the rattle of something in a metal boat. She stiffened in fear. "Terry! Grab that damn thing!" came an urgent whisper. Instinctively, Marly pulled her feet up from the water and rolled onto her stomach, scanning toward the voices. Her aunt's covered boat house blocked her view, so on hands and knees she crept closer for an unobstructed view.

A fear of getting scolded was supplanted by something sinister as her eyes made out the shadows of two men in a flat bottom boat. They had reached the dock of her aunt's neighbor, Marvin Hamby. He was a middle-aged black man who often brought his wife and two kids over from Chattanooga for the weekends. The Hambys had bought the property some years back and developed a friendship with Ginny and Rick.

"Aunt Ginny, how do you know Mr. Marvin?" Marly had once asked.

"We are just neighbors is all."

"Well, we got neighbors, but we don't have them over or do stuff with their kids, and they ain't even black."

Ginny laughed, "Well, lake life is different. You get to know people a little more maybe when you are not having to work and pay bills and all that."

"I like it."

"I like it too, Marly."

And so, the kids were pretty interchangeable, with Rick and Ginny doing the swimming and fishing and the Hambys taking them skiing or tubing. Mr. Hamby had a wooden ski boat of all varnished mahogany and polished metal. "It's a classic," Rick had said once, which seemed to Marly the perfect word to describe the craft.

Marly, her sister, and the Hambys took the boat to the Independence Day flotilla the summer before. The always impeccably dressed Mrs. Hamby wore her hair under a floral scarf to protect it from the winds and had helped Marly tie up her own hair scarf. Riding in "the classic" all dressed up made Marly feel elegant and sophisticated. As they cruised by the "Richie Rich" marina, Mrs. Hamby looked every bit the part of a movie star, and Marly not only knew glamorous as an adjective but as an emotion.

Now, the two men were clambering out of their metal boat onto the Hamby's dock. Hiding in the shadow of her aunt's boathouse, Marly was invisible to them. They went into Mr. Marvin's dock house and set about some business that was a mystery to Marly. "Nothing good is gonna come of that," a corrective phrase her aunt used came to mind and Marly pulled up straight and started running.

The Hambys had wooden steps down to their boat house, but Marly dared not risk coming so close to where the men were. Instead, she crossed diagonally from her aunt's dock to the back door of Mr. Marvin's house. Twigs, rocks and shrubs grabbed for her feet and legs. Her rush up the slope was silent except for her breathing and the shaking of the undergrowth. Still, it was enough to get the attention of the men and one of them stepped out of the boathouse shadows to investigate.

Marly looked back to see him standing on the dock with moonlight ghosting his capped head and broad shoulders. He said to the other still inside, "There's someone up there!"

"Get her!" came a gravelly voice from the darkness. The threat iced her blood and drove her legs faster. With another fleeting look back, she saw the man start bounding up the steps to cut her off. Her heart turned over, but she didn't stray from her course. As she lunged up the hill, something sharp and immovable pierced her foot. Every step after brought up dirt, leaves, and sharper and sharper pain. She believed she could beat the man to the door, but he would no doubt reach her before anyone inside could open it. "Just run away," came a surprisingly reasonable voice from within, but clarity of purpose or perhaps justice dismissed it. She continued sprinting for the Hambys' back door.

Five more steps and both the scrubby brush and dock stairs would end in a small area of lawn. She had a vision of the man tackling her, his large bones breaking her own and powerful hands crushing her throat. There was another impulse to change directions. Instead she screamed into the hushed night, "Mom! Dad! Mom! DAD!"

There was no time and no use looking back now. Twenty yards to the Hambys' back deck, then two more to the back door. A light came on and laid a flat patch of hope across the yard. "Mr. Marvin! Mr. Marvin!" she shouted.

Her bleeding foot hit the first step of the deck and she wanted to leap the rest, to pull her feet high and away from the groping hands trying to stop her. The door opened before she could get there to knock, and a bleary-eyed Mr. Hamby stood there in shabby pajamas with a shotgun in his hand pointed aimlessly at the floor. Five feet from the door Marly leapt straight for his arms and they both tumbled to the floor.

"Good Lord, Marly! Is that you!?"

#

The hospital was bright, hollow and smelled like soap. The sheriff of course had been called and a young deputy with big teeth and thick black hair came by soon after they arrived. He said they had found a can of diesel left on the Hambys' dock and two men in a flat bottom boat on the river fishing. "But they didn't have any fishing poles," the deputy smiled, "or bait." He asked a few questions, but Marly found herself not really wanting to talk anymore. It crossed her mind to challenge the adults, "Do you even know why I was out there?" but she couldn't muster the drama. As the deputy was wrapping up to go she thought to add, "One of them is named Terry."

The deputy flashed his big-toothed grin and took a note. As he was leaving he said, "Thanks. I can't say what they was up to at this point, but I know for a fact that you are a brave young lady." Marly felt her face grow warm but didn't know if it was embarrassment or anger. Aunt Ginny fairly beamed. The deputy left and the doctor came in. Aunt Ginny tried to stay cheerful, but Marly noted the pity and concern that crossed her face when the doctor put in eleven stitches.

--END--

Thank You!

Hopefully, you got a kick, or a surprise, or a hydrangea out of reading *Toward*. Would you consider writing a Review?

Legitimate reviews provide important information for potential readers. Would you take a moment to share your thoughts on this collection?

1. Simply go to the Amazon page for *Toward* at this link: https://tinyurl.com/ya3mva7k

2. Scroll down to the orange button "Write a Customer Review" and click it.

3. Sign in to your Amazon account, and follow the directions to share your thoughts.

About the Author

Troy lives in Petersburg, Tennessee with his wife Margie and two nearly-grown children McKenzie and Harrison. He is a licensed marriage and family therapist with a full-time practice in nearby Fayetteville. He is also an ordained minister in the Cumberland Presbyterian Church and leads the Petersburg congregation.

In 1991 he graduated from Maryville College with a B.A. majoring in Clinical Psychology. From there he would study at Middle Tennessee in the graduate psychology program before completing a masters in Marriage and Family Therapy at Trevecca Nazarene University. In May of 2008, he graduated from Memphis Theological Seminary with a masters of Divinity and received his ordination.

His interests include sports (with a penchant for soccer and Tennessee Volunteer football), competitive online gaming and visual arts such as photography and painting. Since moving to the countryside in 2009, he's developed a strong interest in native plants. You can follow him on Instagram @htroygreen where he shares inspirational messages and images or visit his website to find more of his writings: https://htroygreen.com/

Made in the USA
Middletown, DE
11 April 2018